Portrai..

Andrew Owens

Black Pear Press

Portraits of Prose

Andrew Owens

First published in the UK 2014

Copyright Andrew Owens 2014

All rights reserved.

ISBN 978-1-910322-00-0

Cover art copyright Pauline Owens 2013

Edited by Black Pear Press Limited

The moral right of the author has been asserted.

Introduction

Portraits of Prose is a collection of compelling short stories, each with the power to draw you in and leave a lasting impression. Each tale is concise, unique and well sustained and there is sincerity and feeling in every word. Whether it be the emotionally driven '30 Seconds', the intense and disturbing 'Sinister Justice' or the touching and tender 'Like Mother, Like Daughter', there is something for everyone in this book. With their lovely easy to read style, these insightful stories engage the reader from the first paragraph to the last.

'Delightfully impish' – Glenn James co-founder of 42 Worcester ('No Strings Attached')

'Concise, atmospheric, and with three twists, it engaged and was pretty much a case study in how to get it right' – Gary Longden, Behind the Arras ('Bootleg to Paris')

'Memorable, witty and highly amusing' – Fergus McGonigal ('Between Friends')

'A creepy story with a very surprising twist in the tail' – Jill King, Worcester Writers' Circle ('While We Were Out')

Acknowledgements

Many of the stories in this book have been previously published online, in magazines and anthologies.

Be: Magazine (Worcestershire Literary Festival, 1st Issue November 2011)

The Eerie Digest (www.eeriedigest.com November 2011)

The Survivor's Guide to Bedlam (Wrixon & Hirst & Poets with Voices Strong, 2012)

Five Stop Story Ltd (www.fivestopstory.co.uk February 2013)

42 Worcester (www.42worcester.wordpress.co.uk April 2013)

You Can't Be Serious (Worcester Writers' Circle, 2013)

Short Stories from Black Pear (www.blackpear.net December 2013)

I would like to thank the Worcester Writers' Circle, the Worcestershire Literary Festival and 42 Worcester for providing a platform for these stories to be expressed. I would also like to thank my publishers Black Pear Press for their tireless work on my behalf. They have been both an inspiration and good friends.

Dedicated to my wife Samantha, my sons
Cameron and Matthew and my daughter Louise

Table of Contents

30 Seconds

'Martin! Martin!'

My wife says, when you have three kids, you have to have eyes on the back of your head. Thirty seconds, that's how long it takes for a parent to lose a child.

'Martin! Martin!' In a shop full of people, my voice cut the air like there was nobody there. I pushed the pushchair close to the till and stood by the only exit of the video rental shop.

'Charlie, go look for your brother,' I told my eldest son. It was blind hope; I knew Martin would have answered my call if he'd heard me.

'Martin!' I called, peering in-between aisles by the entrance. The shop was empty.

'He's not here, Dad,' Charlie said.

'Stay here with your sister. If you see Martin, tell him to stay here,' I said walking towards the back of the shop.

'He's not there, sir. He's not anywhere in the shop,' the shop assistant said. 'Why don't you leave the other two with me and have a look in the stationery store across the car park? They'll be alright. These two will be fine.'

These two will be fine, great. And what about the third? Life without Martin? It didn't bear thinking about and yet it was there in my mind. He won't be there. He wouldn't just run off, I thought as I left the video shop. The doors were wide open to let the cool summer breeze in and there was a line of cars parked just a couple of feet from the entrance. A horrible thought flashed in my mind. Man grabs kid, walks straight outdoors, into car, gone. The hopelessness of that possibility worried me. We'd never get him back. I simply couldn't accept that thought, but, as Martin had never wandered off before, there was no other explanation.

'Have you got CCTV?' I asked the shop assistant.

'No… sorry.'

'Dad, they've got Bash and Eruptor!' Charlie exclaimed.

'Great, Charlie. Excellent,' I replied, resting my hands on my knees and taking deep breaths.

'Come on over here with your sister and me and tell me all about it. Your dad's a bit busy.'

'Okay, I'm going to look over the road. Charlie, be good and stay here in the shop with Lauren.'

My fear was increasing with every passing minute. Martin wouldn't randomly walk into a shop across the road on his own, but where else could I look? The possibilities were limited and I was becoming desperate.

I approached two members of staff in the stationery superstore and told them of the situation and my missing son's name. Martin was soon announced over the tannoy, while a third employee scouted around the store. I told the staff that I would be at the video shop should they find him.

I gazed through the open door from the car park and could see Charlie and Lauren with the video shop assistant. At least they were being good. Still no sign of Martin. It was time to ring my wife. She was out with her mother. I dreaded telling her that I'd lost our son.

'The person you are calling is unable to take your call. Please leave your message after the tone.'

'Come on, pick up,' I said, trying again. As expected, no luck. I know, I'll try her mum.

'The person you are calling...'

'What's your son's name again?' a woman asked me, as I put my mobile into my top pocket.

'Martin,' I replied, and before I could say another word she walked off in search of my son.

If I were Martin and lost, what would I do? Where would I go? Home. I could trust Charlie to find his way home on his own, but Martin? I wasn't so sure. Home was something I didn't want to contemplate. To me, to head back was to admit defeat and how could I return without him?

'You guys alright?' I said, checking on Charlie and Lauren. The shop assistant had given them a handful of jellies each to keep them amused for the time being. 'Thanks, how much do I owe you for the sweets?'

'You don't.'

I smiled at her and said, 'I'm going to go and have a look by the canal.'

'Do you want me to call the police?' she asked.

'Yeah.'

Walking across the car park in the direction of the canal, I was stopped by a middle-aged couple walking in the opposite direction. Like the woman who had asked for my son's name, they too had been in the video shop and had left to join the search.

'He's not by the canal and we've just come back from DIY and the pizza house. My wife's going to check out the mobile store and I'm going to have a look on the other side of the bridge.'

Though I appreciated their help, I couldn't even muster a thank you. It was looking increasingly unlikely that I would ever see my son again. My head ached, my vision began to blur. I couldn't think what to do next.

'Excuse me, sir. The police would like to take a few details,' the shop assistant called to me from the open doorway. As I walked back to the video shop, she met me halfway and handed me the phone.

'Hello?'

'Yes hi, could you please tell me your son's name and how old he is?' the officer asked.

'His name is Martin Aldrich and he's six. It was his birthday just the other day.'

'Can you describe him for me, Mr Aldrich? What was he wearing, jeans?'

'Yes, he was wearing jeans and a light blue hooded jumper. He has dirty blond hair, rather short because it was cut recently and he is quite tall for his age.'

'How tall? Three feet? Does he have any distinct features?'

He has a chicken pox scar on his eyelid, I thought, but it's not like anyone is going to see it and as for his height, I've never measured him, I haven't got a clue. Any distinct features? I could be describing just about anyone's kid.

'No,' I replied.

'Try not to worry, sir. I'm sure he hasn't gotten too far. We'll find him.'

'Found him. Some lady's bringing him down the hill.'

Oh, the relief! I ran towards them. I could see that Martin was fine. On seeing me, his face changed; he looked embarrassed.

'He was at the top of the hill, by the traffic lights,' the old lady said, still holding Martin's hand. 'He asked me if I knew his dad, then he said you were at the video shop.'

I thanked the old lady, who smiled and held Martin's hand out to me. I took his hand as if I'd never let it go again.

Back in the video store, Charlie gave Martin a few of the jellies he had saved for him and then I asked him why he'd left the shop. He couldn't answer me; his lower lip trembled and tears formed in his eyes. I pulled him close and rubbed his head.

'Don't worry, I'm not angry,' I reassured him. 'I was scared. Let's go into town and see if we can find a cake to take home with us.'

Soon Martin was smiling and nothing more was said. Martin didn't want to let go of my hand and I didn't want to let go of his.

Thirty seconds, that's how long it takes to lose a child. Just thirty seconds.

All Inclusive

'Yeah hi, I'm calling in regards to the ad in the paper.'

'And which ad would that be for, sir?'

'The all inclusive wedding package for £3000. I was wondering if you could tell me a bit more about it.'

'Yes certainly. We provide a service for a civil ceremony in the Harriet Hall, the wedding breakfast would take place in the business lounge and the evening reception would be in the Letterworth Suite. Both the civil ceremony and the breakfast would be for fifty guests and the evening reception for seventy, but you could add to those numbers if necessary. When were you planning on holding the wedding?'

'I'm in no rush. I've waited this long. When could you do it?'

'No earlier than next year. If you are looking to hold a summer wedding, the first two weekends in July are fully booked and so is the first weekend in August.'

'Fine. So, when would I meet her?'

'Uh, who?'

'My wife.'

'Excuse me, your wife?'

'Yes, my wife. Would I get to meet her before the wedding or on the day? I'm not fussy. I've not had so much as a girlfriend before now so I don't really care what she looks like.'

'This is some kind of a joke, right?'

'This is no laughing matter. You mean to say that you don't provide partners for single customers?'

'No, we don't.'

'Well, your ad did say 'everything you need for your wedding day' and I need a wife. Uh, hello? Hello?'

Between Friends

She straddled my lap. One leg knelt on the bench, the other propped on its arm, Michelle rode up and down on me, panting with excitement. There was no time to lose. Her boyfriend, Kevin, would be back in fifteen minutes and that didn't give us a lot of time to conceal the evidence.

I had dreamt of this moment for months. Ever since I had first met her at a friend's party, I longed for her. She was beautiful and intelligent with a great sense of humour. Her dress sense was enticing, not sleazy and something about her pulled me towards her. Michelle was everything I wanted in a woman except for one thing; she was my best friend's girl.

Lips locked and pulse racing, the fear of being caught, not just by Kevin, but by the Sunday bar staff that need only to look in the smoking area alcove to find us, was exhilarating. Upping the tempo, it took all of my will to satisfy her. As our peaks matched, we kissed at the tailing off of our crescendo.

Straightening herself up, Michelle said with a smile, 'That was great.'

I leant back on the bench, fastened my belt and replied, 'It sure was.'

'Now you can have a smoke,' my cheeky lover said, doing up her blouse. 'I'm going to the ladies. Meet you in the bar.'

I put a cigarette in my mouth and smiled. We may have sinned, but it felt so right. She told me she had wanted me for a long time.

It had been the first time we had been left alone together. Not that we'd given Kevin any reason to be suspicious. The opportunity to be alone had just not arisen.

We had all gone to catch a jam session at a pub in the city. The event boasted some of the best upcoming bands in the area. We had got there a couple of hours early, so we could have a few drinks before the show. Shortly after our arrival, Kevin left, saying he had a few things to do and would be back in an hour.

Alone, Michelle and I sat down, had a drink, joked and flirted. A few minutes later, I excused myself to have a cigarette. She followed. Taking a fag from my pocket, she stopped me from lighting it and said, 'Not just yet.' She kissed me and I pulled her in close, seizing on the moment.

I put out my cigarette and rejoined the pub's patrons in the bar. I noted Kevin stood at the counter ordering a drink. Looking to the table where we once sat, I could see Michelle. She gave me a reassuring smile and beckoned me over. Sitting across from her I picked up my beer.

'I was here when he walked in. No need to worry,' Michelle whispered. I could see that she still looked slightly flushed, but thought it would go unnoticed by anyone else.

Returning from the bar, Kevin took a seat next to Michelle and she put her arm in his. He neither spoke nor acknowledged my return from the smoking area. Something wasn't right. Kevin appeared distracted. When the opening act took to the stage, he seemed disinterested. Did he suspect? If he did, he wasn't saying anything and my best friend wasn't one to hold back on his anger.

I felt a gentle touch on the inside of my leg. I looked at Michelle in surprise and she winked, continuing to arouse my interest with a subtle stroke of her foot along my calf. I smiled and made like I was interested in the show, praying that Kevin wouldn't notice what was going on under the table.

'Anyone need a drink?' Kevin asked, getting up to go to the bar. Michelle and I passed on the offer and he looked like he couldn't care less.

'What's wrong with him?' I asked, leaning across the table.

'He's been offish all week. I'm sick of it. I'm leaving him, Danny. I want you.'

For the next hour we sat in silence. I was sure that none of us was interested in the band. My thoughts were between my desire for Michelle and my concern for Kevin. It was time for a smoke.

I had just got up to leave, when Michelle announced that she needed to visit the loo. We met in the corridor between the smoking area and the toilets and embraced for a moment.

It was just in passing, but the memory of it lasted well after my return to the bar.

The silence resumed. Kevin hardly spoke and was quiet even after we left to catch the train. I couldn't be sure if he was angry or upset, but I did notice that he and Michelle were not holding hands.

Fortunately, we didn't have to wait long at the station, and in ten minutes we boarded the train. I took a seat across from Michelle; Kevin sat next to her.

Twenty minutes into the journey and Kevin got up to go to the toilet. No sooner had he left, than Michelle started to come on to me.

Slipping off one of her heels, Michelle stuck her foot between my legs and began to rub. It felt wonderful and, like when we were on the bench in the smoking area, the worry of being found out added to the thrill.

Glancing to my right, I noticed a middle-aged woman staring at us. She glared with disapproval. Michelle smiled at her and gave her a cheeky wave, briefly ceasing with my intimate massage. A couple of minutes later, Michelle removed her foot and slipped it back into her shoe. Kevin came back and though he looked no happier, I was sure he was none the wiser.

For a time I worried that the disapproving woman might say something, but once we got off the train I stopped worrying. We had arrived at our stop forty-five minutes after departing from the city. It was 11:30pm, time to go our separate ways.

Kevin and I both lived close to the station, but Michelle lived on the other side of town, so we walked her to the taxi rank. Kevin said goodbye, but Michelle thanked only me for the time we had spent together. We watched her cab drive off from the traffic lights.

Alone with Kevin, I turned and faced my friend. His expression was no longer like a sad lost puppy, his face was long and his eyes were red. He was welling up and looked as though he was about to lose it.

'We need to talk.'

Shit, he knows about me and Michelle. Keep calm. Don't do anything to provoke him.

Suddenly, Kevin broke down crying. He put his hands on his head and knelt down on the path at the side of the road. Confused, I asked, 'Kevin, are you alright?'

'No, no I'm not.'

'What's wrong?'

'I've cheated on her.'

Stunned, I replied, 'What?'

'I cheated on Michelle.'

'When?'

'Three months ago, when she was out with her friends and you were away visiting family.'

'How? Why?'

'I went to this party and met this girl. I was drunk, one thing led to another and... I can't live with myself. I've got to tell her, Danny. What should I do?'

Part of me wanted Kevin to admit what he'd done to Michelle. She was sure to dump him and we would be open to seeing each other. But he was my best friend and to let him own up without offering him any sort of advice would be out of character, plus she told me she was going to leave him anyway.

'Don't tell her. Keep it to yourself. What she doesn't know won't hurt her. Get yourself back on track. You can get through this. You'll thank me one day. Trust me.'

Kevin leant back against the station wall and looked up at me. His eyes were streaming with tears, his bottom lip quivering, his body shaking.

'I have to tell her,' he blurted out, 'I haven't got a choice. I've got syphilis, Danny! I've got fucking syphilis!'

Wordless, I staggered from the station, leaving my friend at the side of the road. He called out to me several times, but my mind was in such a muddle I couldn't register what he was saying. It didn't matter, for even if I'd heard, I wouldn't have been listening.

Bootleg to Paris

Passport, check. Ticket, check. Just enough time for a cigarette before I enter Departures.

I swapped my passport and ticket for my pack of *Marlboro Lights* and rifled through my handbag for my elusive lighter. Suddenly, a short flame appeared in front of me. I glanced upward as I leaned forward to accept the light from the accommodating stranger.

The man before me was tall, looked twice my age with thinning hair. He was tanned much like myself. Smartly dressed in a dark blue, pinstriped suit with a matching tie, he looked like a businessman. After exhaling the first drag of my cigarette, I smiled and said 'Muito obrigado.'

'De rien,' he replied.

Caught by surprise, I looked attentively towards him. He was French like me, but I had spoken in Portuguese. How did he know? I could see he'd noted my puzzlement.

'Your dress sense is very European and there is a fleur de lis on your jacket,' he said. 'You speak Portuguese well.'

'My mother is Brazilian and my father is French.'

'Visiting family here in Rio?'

'Petropolis.'

'Ah, Petropolis. Not staying for Festas Juninas?'

'No.' He was asking too many questions and I was in no mood to answer them. I threw my cigarette to the ground. 'It was nice meeting you. Must check in.'

I looked through my messages on my mobile, as I waited in the queue for my turn to pass through the security scanner. There was a text from my associate, Edward. It said, 'C U Tues at café. Av a gud flight.'

Though he didn't say, I knew he was eager to get the package I had in my rucksack. Coke, two hundred grams inside three cans of coffee. I wasn't worried about getting it past security. This was my fifth trip in eighteen months. Even when I set off the scanner I wasn't concerned. The metal detector always manages to find something and this time it was the studs on my belt. However, I soon had reason to be alarmed.

I stood with my arms outstretched as a female security guard waved a handheld detector over me. One of her colleagues began to search through my bag. Sure enough, the young security man pulled out two of the tins I was carrying.

'What's this?' he asked abruptly.

'Coffee,' I said with as much confidence as I could, careful not to seem condescending.

'I can see that. Why three?'

'One for my mother, one for my brother and his wife and one for myself.'

I think the fact that the cans were sealed and that I spoke fluent Portuguese helped. The security man put the coffee back into the bag and, to my relief, I was soon on my way. There's usually some sort of glitch when bootlegging drugs and I was convinced that was it.

Half an hour to boarding and I was standing in a bookshop looking for a newspaper. My mom always asked me to take her one home whenever I was in Brazil. There wasn't much of a headline story, but so long as it was near to the departure date, she would be happy.

Casually checking the date, I thought about getting some chocolate for the journey home. Taking a chocolate bar and a roll of mints to the till, I noticed that the man standing ahead of me was the stranger who had given me a light. He smiled, said nothing, paid for his bottled water and bag of sweets and went towards gates G to M.

'Now boarding... flight... to Paris at Gate J13.' I heard the call for my flight as I left the shop. The queue of passengers wasn't moving; those with children or special needs would be seated first, so I took a seat close to the window. I saw the plane I would soon be boarding and viewed the early evening horizon. The sun was setting; I wouldn't see it again until landing in France.

After the initial boarding of passengers, I was soon walking down the tunnel to the plane. Jostling between travellers loading their hand luggage into the overhead compartments, I found my window seat. There was one vacant seat beside it.

I placed my rucksack by my feet and settled into my standard recliner, took out my mobile and wrote a couple of last-minute texts. The first was to my brother, Beniot, who would be collecting me when I landed. The next was to Edward.

'On plane takeoff soon. Hols went well. Got ur souvenir. Look forward 2 gettin back. C U Tues.'

I leaned down, unzipped the front pocket of my rucksack and placed my phone inside. I sat up and saw the person allocated to the seat beside me was the stranger.

'What a delightful coincidence,' he said, closing the catch to the overhead compartment before sitting down beside me. Extending his hand he leaned towards me. 'Pierre.'

'Renee,' I returned, accepting his hand, trying my best to hide my unease. This was weird and most disconcerting. Surely he wasn't…Nah. I was just being paranoid. Three months ago I was convinced that a car had tailed me from Charles de Gaulle to home and that had come to nothing.

'Nice to meet you again, Renee. I'm sure we will have plenty of time to properly introduce ourselves over the course of the flight. I do so hate lift-offs and landings,' he said, leaning back in his seat. Fifteen minutes later the plane was off the ground.

An hour into the flight and the plane had settled out into its steady flight path, and the airline's staff began to prepare for the first in-flight service. The pilot's voice came over the speaker, explaining that we would be landing in Paris in eleven hours, and the seatbelt indicator had turned off.

I was about to dig out the newspaper I had bought for my mother, when Pierre leaned over towards me once again. He smiled and it looked like he was going to tell me more than his name and where he lived. God, I hope he isn't going to be one of those people who suddenly take it upon themselves to talk shit and tell you all about their life history.

Speaking in a warm and serene manner Pierre said, 'Well, I guess we're on our way.'

Yeah, no shit. Here we go.

'It will be straight back to work for me when we land. How about you, Miss Turgeon?'

I started to shake with fright and alarm. He knew my surname but how could he? I felt the blood drain from my face and looked intently at him. He no longer smiled. His face seemed sinister. I remained rigid and mute and he spoke to me in a clear but low tone.

'My name is Pierre Lemieux, Special Constable Lemieux. We know what you're up to, Miss Turgeon, and there's a car waiting to take you back to the station when we land. You're going to go down for a very long time, Renee, but if you cooperate, we can help to reduce your sentence. If you tell us who your contact is and help us with his arrest, I am sure we can make your stay at Fresnes less unpleasant. Who's your contact?'

I couldn't speak. My head felt like a whirlwind and it took all the strength I had to maintain a cool exterior. What do I do? What should I say? PC Lemieux was hardly going to let me walk and he was expecting an answer.

'Who's your contact, Renee? The sooner you tell me the easier it will be. What do you say?'

I leant down to my rucksack and retrieved my headphones and plugged them into the armrest. Pierre leaned closer until we were nose to nose. 'That's right, you think on it. In just over nine hours we'll be landing and you'll have plenty of time to consider the error of your ways, even more so if you keep this up.'

He sat back and I turned and faced the window. There was nothing to see, only the blackness of night and a beacon of light from the aircraft's wing. I was angry, and helpless. I was on my way to prison and yet it felt like I was already there, restricted to my surroundings and left to ponder my sins.

An hour later and my silence was interrupted by one of the cabin crew who pushed a trolley carrying tea and coffee. 'Is there anything I can get you?' she asked.

Pierre spoke first, 'Coffee, please.'

'Yes,' I said, 'another seat would be nice.'

'Is there a problem?' she asked, then saw my expression, 'I'll see what I can do.'

Leaning towards me, Pierre said, 'You won't be moving.'

All of a sudden, the plane started to shake violently. It was like the tremor of an earthquake except we weren't on solid ground. It stopped momentarily then shook again. Pierre spilled the remains of his drink into the gangway. I could see flashes of lightning out the window. The fasten seatbelts sign came on and the pilot interrupted the music on my headset.

'We are passing through an area of turbulence which should not last for too long. Please remain seated and I will keep you posted.'

Pierre looked white when the plane dropped several hundred feet a few minutes later. The engines stalled and passengers began to scream. For a moment, the pilot seemed to regain control of the craft, but it was only for a brief time. The plane was plummeting towards the ocean at a phenomenal speed. There was no time to act or speak. I knew within a few short minutes we would all be dead, and so did Pierre.

I'm not one to pray and I don't believe in god, so there was no chance of divine intervention. I wasn't one to rely on luck either, so it would seem that my fate was sealed. At least, I thought, I wouldn't be going to prison.

By Invitation

'Are you sure this is the place?' I asked my girlfriend, Ruth.

'Well, it says so on the card,' she replied, shrugging her shoulders.

'It can't be?' I looked at the disused shop unsure what to do. The window was frosted over and there was no sign above it. The only thing to validate that we had come to the right address was the number plaque.

'Try the door,' Ruth suggested.

'It's open,' I said, turning to her in amazement.

She gestured. 'Well, go on then.'

I pushed the door forward and together we stepped into the vacant shop. The bell above the door announced our arrival, echoing through a room strewn with newspaper and tins of paint. Apart from a counter set along the back wall, the room was bare of furnishings.

'There's no one here. Let's go,' I said, reopening the door, the bell above my head ringing out again.

'There's a door behind the counter. Perhaps they didn't hear us,' Ruth replied, walking into the dust-covered expanse.

'Ruth, let's go. This hardly looks like the kind of place to hold a spiritual healing event. The address on the card must be a misprint. Maybe it's Maple Avenue not Maple Street?' Ruth ignored me, making her way to the door behind the counter. She tried the handle and sure enough the door opened.

'Keith, come here. Have a look at this.'

I walked past the dusty counter and joined Ruth in the next room. It was much the same as the shop floor, with bits of cardboard, the odd nail and a few tins scattered about. There was also an archway leading to an equally unremarkable room in the middle of the back wall, but it was the closed wooden door to the left of it that had grabbed her attention. In a store stripped clean of all decor, there in the centre of the whitewashed door was a large symbol, scrawled in red paint. With its slapdash appearance, it could almost be mistaken for graffiti; it was too symmetrical to be called a scribble. I had no idea what it was trying to depict, but it made me feel most uncomfortable.

'What is it?' Ruth asked.

'I don't know and I don't care. Come on, we're wasting our time. Let's go back to the car. We can get a pizza and watch something on TV.'

'But I told Kate that we'd see her.'

'Phone her. I'm sure she'll understand.'

Ruth nodded and then took her mobile out from her handbag. Putting it to her ear, she paced about the room. She stopped pacing a few seconds later, standing before the curiously marked door. She had a puzzled look on her face.

'It's cut into the answer service. I'm going to try again.'

'What for?'

'Well, I can't be sure, but I thought I heard the faint sound of a phone ringing on the other side of this door.'

With one ear on her phone and the other pressed against the door, Ruth listened intently for her best friend's ringtone. For a couple of seconds the room was deathly silent, but then Ruth stepped away from the door. She suddenly looked pale as she turned to me for reassurance.

'Listen, can you hear it?'

I put my ear to the door. Sure enough I could hear the chime of somebody's mobile.

'It is, isn't it?' she asked.

I moved towards her and put her hand in mine. I could immediately sense her unease on taking it.

'It might not be hers,' I said. Ruth didn't look convinced.

'Right, someone is ringing at the same time as I am?'

'It's possible,' I replied.

'Not likely. Either way, we've got to go in there. I need to see for myself. I need to know.'

Ruth gave me an insistent glare. I took hold of the handle and pulled the door towards me. A waft of cold air escaped from beyond and was followed by a forbidding creak as the door scraped over the concrete. Its ghostly welcome put a shiver down my spine and I'm not someone who can be scared easily. The stairway was dark, but there down in the distance was a dim orange glow coming from somewhere off to the right.

'After you,' Ruth said, still quivering.

'Fuck that,' I replied, taking a step back, 'I ain't going down there.'

'Keith, you've got to. It's Kate's phone. I know it is and she might need our help.'

I swallowed hard before taking to the stairs. I crept slowly and each step that creaked raised the level of my angst. The only support I had was Ruth's presence; her hand had taken residence on my shoulder.

The chill in the air was more prominent at the base of the stairs and the cellar was masked in darkness. The only thing visible was the gleam from the archway a few feet ahead. In spite of its light, I didn't feel comforted and I could tell Ruth felt the same as she took hold of my arm.

Peering around the corner, I felt both relieved and alarmed. The narrow room beyond was vacant but disturbing. The source of the light was a lantern set on a wooden table and beside it were a purse and a mobile phone. However, set in the far wall was a solid steel door with a closed shutter. Combined with the stonework, the cramped chamber had the look of a feudal dungeon.

I led Ruth into the room and she went straight to the table to look through the purse and to collect the mobile phone. I went to the forbidding door and opened the shutter. It took a few seconds to adjust to the difference in light, but eventually I was able to see inside. There, bound to a chair with a gag in her mouth, was Ruth's best friend, Kate. On seeing my eyes, Kate's widened and she began to wobble about her seat.

'It is Kate's phone!' Ruth exclaimed.

'I know. She's in here. Are there any keys on that table?'

'I can't see any. Maybe they're in the other room.'

There wasn't a light switch on any of the walls that I could see, so I walked over to the archway and ran my hands along the stonework.

'Ah, here we go,' I said turning on the light.

As my eyes adjusted to the light, five figures appeared in front of me. They were dressed in matching robes and they each looked gaunt, but most disturbing of all were their eyes. They were rolled back, showing the whites, but somehow I sensed they could see.

An overwhelming need to leave the cellar consumed me. I reached back, took hold of Ruth's arm and tried to pull her towards me, but she didn't move. I turned to face her and met with her lifeless eyes. She was one of them.

Cocksure

There she was, stood at the end of the bar, looking real hot. She was wearing heels, a low cut top and a skirt that was more like a belt. Her breasts were large, perky and I could care less if they were fake. I couldn't get the thought of them out of my head, smothering my face.

She had caught my eye earlier. She was with three of her friends and they all appeared to be single. They danced around their handbags and took it in turns to buy drinks. Now it was her round, the best opportunity for me to make my move.

Strutting across the open floor like a peacock in full plume, I made my way towards her. Jigging to the beat with drink in hand, I was psyched and ready to slide on up and hit her with a killer line. Confidence is everything and I was poised. She looked sleazy, easy, a real man-eater and I had that something she wanted.

'Hi, can I borrow your phone? I need to call God and tell him that I found his missing angel.'

I could tell by her reaction that I was in. She smiled, winked and then licked her lips. She turned towards me and tugged at her skirt.

'Grrrr, yer fit. Fancy a shag, bab? I got the all clear yesterday. The crabs are all gone now and I'm just itching for another ride!'

'Sorry,' I replied, 'I thought you were somebody else.'

Dancing Apart

Lying naked next to one another, engrossed in the film on TV, my girlfriend and I were watching Patrick Swayze teach Jennifer Grey how to dance from the comfort of our bed. Neither of us had spoken since the start of the film. Dirty Dancing was her all-time favourite and I was wrapped up in my thoughts.

It had been the first time we had made love in five weeks, surprising when you consider that the majority of the first month of our relationship had been spent under the sheets. I had often made suggestions to adjourn to the bedroom, but to no avail and after three weeks of unsuccessful pleading, I gave up on trying. Even on this occasion, the sex hadn't been great. It had only happened because she had wanted it and once the moment had passed, her interest had changed much like her affection. There was no pillow talk or cuddles afterwards and there was certainly no chance of prompting her for a second or third session, which had been effortless in the past. No, on went the TV and in went her favourite film with no consultation as to what I might like to watch.

Plenty of unanswered questions were springing to mind. Is there something you're not telling me? Why make love and then give me the cold shoulder? Have I done something wrong? Had it gone like this with her previous boyfriend, who she had been with for just over two years?

I didn't know that much about Sheryl's previous partner, Alex. I only met him twice and both times had been brief. He was a high school dropout and came from a very rough neighbourhood, but in spite of his background he seemed nice enough and Sheryl had never told me any tales of domestic abuse. She only said that he had issues with jealousy and that she suspected that he had had an affair with another woman. It was time to find out more, but I'd have to be indirect if I was going to avoid another argument.

'Sher...'

'Hmm,' she replied.

'Did you ever try and watch this with Alex?'

'Yes, but he'd soon lose interest,' she returned, without turning to acknowledge me.

'What do you mean?'

'He'd just walk out and turn the TV on in the front room or go to the garage and do some work on his car. Why?' Sheryl asked, turning towards me.

'No reason, just wondering. Did you ever try to watch something together that he'd want?'

'Woo, football, great! He only liked to watch sports or boring documentaries. Anymore questions you'd like to ask?' She glared at me.

Feeling dead inside, I pondered, why does it feel like hard work to keep this relationship going, surely it should be easy? It's like you're avoiding the issues we have and putting the onus of guilt solely on my shoulders. Why can't we talk? When we do talk, I'm never in the right or I'm left to feel as though I'm overreacting. Do you really love me? I was afraid to ask.

The uncertainty of her devotion was pulling me apart, but I was scared to leave. Is this it? Is this what love is? What if there isn't that someone special out there waiting for me? If I call it a day, would I be destined to walk this earth alone? Time seems to pass so slowly when you're on your own and life seems so meaningless. Can I make this work? Do I want to make this work? Will I ever know?

I needed a distraction. Sheryl was not about to sit and talk and if I got up and left the room to do something else, I'd be setting myself up to be compared to Alex. I'd have to watch the film. Not my sort of movie, but then again, how bad could it be?

'Have you had many women?' Grey asks Swayze, lying naked on his chest.

'What?' Swayze replies, looking uneasy.

'Have you had many women?' she says, still sporting a smile that projects her innocence.

'Baby, come on.'

'Tell me. I want to know.'

'No, no,' Swayze returns, jumping out of bed.

Like Patrick Swayze, I too began to feel ever more uncomfortable. The scene instantly reminded me of a conversation I once had with Sheryl, but unlike Patrick she didn't attempt to explain. Sheryl was my first and when we met I believed she would be my only, but now my sight was returning with stark reality.

'That's the thing, Baby, you see? It wasn't like that. They were using me.'

I couldn't sit in silence anymore. I had to know.

'Why did you kick Alex out?'

'What?' Sheryl replied, caught off guard by my random query.

'Why did you kick Alex out? What did he do that told you enough was enough?'

'He didn't get me anything for Valentine's Day. No card, no present and no plans to go out. He had made no effort at all.'

Suddenly, I was hit by a revelation, a comprehension of what had previously been misunderstood. Sheryl didn't know it, but she'd confirmed the suspicions that were troubling me. Jumping out of bed, I began to get dressed.

'What are you doing?' Sheryl asked, sitting upright.

'Valentine's Day? You kicked Alex out on Valentine's Day?'

'That's right, so?'

'You phoned and asked me out the very next day. You didn't wait long to get over Alex did you? You made me believe that you and Alex had broke up at least a month before we started going out. I thought you were so happy because I was giving you the kind of love and attention that you never had before. You made me believe that I was special, but instead you took advantage of my naivety. You used me to get over Alex. I thought you loved me, but in actual fact I didn't matter at all and ever since we met you've abused my trust and kindness to see how much you could get.'

Sheryl sat soundless with a smug look on her face. She made no attempt to apologise or plead with me to stay.

Instead, she watched me put on my shoes and collect a few personal items in silence, before I walked out of the room and out of her flat without so much as a goodbye. It was over and I was furious.

Living back with my parents, two weeks had passed and I had heard nothing from Sheryl. I was getting ready to go out to meet my friends at JP's pool hall, when there was a knock at the door that my mother answered.

'Ed, there's someone at the door for you,' my mum said, stepping back into the kitchen before mouthing the words, 'It's Sheryl.'

Pulling on my shirt and grabbing my wallet and keys from the table, I walked past my mum and over to the door. Sheryl stood on the doorstep with a beaming smile. I said nothing, allowing her to say what she was eager to tell me.

'I've decided to move up north to become closer to my family. I can continue with my studies up there and I can get away from the things like Alex and everything else that's been holding me back. I think it'll be good for me.'

'So do I.' Before Sheryl could say another word, I walked straight past her, got into my car and drove off, leaving her on the doorstep with my mother.

Fatal Insight

Crash! The sound of the collision shook me throughout and it took several seconds for me to realise what had happened.

I turned away from the cash point to see a large grey saloon with a huge dent in the front bumper and buckled hood. Though he appeared uninjured, the driver looked to be in shock.

I could see the remains of a sports-bike in the middle of the street. Bits of the mangled metal were strewn about the road. The contorted, leather-clad rider lay still a few yards to the left of the ruined vehicle. I knew he was in a bad way.

As I walked towards the rider, a bystander said, 'He's dead.' His face was shrouded by the cracked helmet.

Beep! Beep! Beep!

I shot out of bed and switched off the alarm. I woke in a cold sweat. This wasn't the first time I had had such a vivid dream.

I reached for my mobile by the bedside table and began to text my sister. It was Friday and I would be off work early, so we could easily meet up at a café before she needed to pick up her kids from school. Liz was the only person I could talk to, the only one who would believe me.

Standing up from the table, I greeted my sister with a peck on the cheek.

'This is nice,' she said, as we both sat down. 'Haven't seen you in ages and come Sunday it will be twice in three days.'

'Why? What's on Sunday?' I asked.

'Mum's birthday. Please tell me you haven't forgotten? You've at least got her a card, right?'

'This Sunday? Damn.' I'd forgotten again, as always.

'I knew you wouldn't, so I got you this card to sign.'

Breathing a sigh, I said, 'You're a good one, Sis.'

'I'll leave it up to you to get her a present.' My sister smiled.

'I'll make sure I get her something after we leave here.'

My sister's glance made me turn to the left where a young man, one of the cafe staff, waited for us to finish with our conversation before taking our order.

'What can I get you both?'

'I'll have a tea and a Belgian Bun,' Liz answered.

'I'll have the same, but with a coffee, please,' I replied.

'So, why are we here? What's this all about?' Liz asked, leaning forward.

I paused for a moment and looked about the room. The café was busy and all were preoccupied with their own conversations. I looked back at my sister and met her curious gaze.

'It's happening again,' I said.

'What's happening again, Ron?' Liz asked, with a raised eyebrow.

'The dreams. Remember ten years ago when I told you that I had dreamt about someone dying in an industrial accident?'

'Yes.'

'...but I couldn't see his face, and then three days later, after Dad died...'

'Yes.'

'Well, have a look at this,' I said, handing my sister a clipping from yesterday's edition of The Times.

She took a few seconds to read it, 'Bank manager found dead in her home. Police not treating it as suspicious. So?'

'Last week I went to the bank to secure a loan. I was introduced to this lady; we went through a few details and set up the loan. That was that, or so I thought,' I said, shifting in my seat. I glanced about the room before continuing, 'Two nights later, I dreamt that I was in this strange house. I went up the stairs and I could see steam coming from the gap under a door. I tried the handle and the door opened. It was then that I saw a most horrific sight. Lying in the bath was a woman with her head tilted back, her arms draped over the sides and a pool of blood beside the tub. But I couldn't see her face. As hard as I tried, I couldn't make out who she was and I didn't make the connection until I had read it in the paper.'

'There are plenty of bankers in this city, how can you be sure it was the one you saw?' Liz asked.

I handed her the business card I had been given. She stared at the standard Royal Bank issue and compared it with the news clipping. 'Fiona Walker – Branch Manager'/ 'Fiona Walker, 32, local bank manager'.

'Last night I dreamt that I had seen a terrible accident where a motorcyclist was killed. I couldn't see his face. If only I knew who he was, I could warn him, Liz.'

'Perhaps it's because you don't know them,' Liz said, 'or maybe it's because you're not meant to, who knows?' Now Liz stared intently at me. 'Don't go beating yourself up, Ron. There's nothing you can do.'

I nodded. I was stressed out by my dreams, but Liz had managed to comfort me by listening and not calling me mad. We finished our drinks and I paid the bill. We left the café and I walked my sister to her car.

'It was lovely to see you, Liz, thanks for listening. We'll have to do it again soon,' I said, taking a cigarette out from my jacket.

'Smoking again?' she said, looking into the packet. There were six cigarettes left in my pack of twenty. Liz didn't say anything. Her expression said it all.

Getting into her car, she spoke to me through the open window, 'If you have any more of these dreams, give me a call. See you Sunday.'

'Yeah, see you Sunday.'

I walked down the street in a world of my own. Suddenly, a thought jumped into my head. Sunday, Mum's birthday! I had to get her a present. I still had a few minutes left on the meter and had to get something while it was still fresh in my mind. Better get some money first. I threw my cigarette butt to the ground and went to the first cash point I came to and inserted my card.

Crash! My heart stopped. I didn't need to turn around; I could already guess what had happened. I turned and gazed at the scene behind me. There before me was a large grey saloon, the ruins of a sports-bike and its contorted rider on the ground.

I walked over to where the victim lay. A bystander said, 'He's dead.'

I looked down at the rider and gasped. I was horrified to see his visor didn't hide his identity as it had in my dream. There before me was the body of the waiter who had served me and my sister only an hour before. A shiver ran over me and I walked away quickly.

That night I tossed and turned in bed. I couldn't switch off and put the motionless face of the waiter out of my mind. I looked at my alarm clock. It was 3:31am. The alarm was set for seven and though I didn't need to get up for work, I was determined to go back into town to get my mum the present I'd forgotten on so many previous birthdays.

Standing near the counter of a convenience store, I saw Liz. She had a pained expression I had never seen before. She was silent and looked sad and shaken.

Beep! Beep! Beep!

I shot out of bed and fumbled about for my mobile. Picking it up, I texted Liz. The vividness of my latest dream made me want to send it as soon as I could. I waited for her to text a reply and to my relief the phone chimed less than ten minutes later. Her text said, 'C U @ café when it opens'. I didn't bother with breakfast; I went straight into town as soon as I was dressed.

Standing outside the café, with a cigarette in one hand and a small shopping bag in the other, I waited for Liz to arrive. As I cast the stub into the road, I saw my sister and walked over to her. I felt all on edge; the cigarette had done nothing to calm my nerves.

'Ron, you look terrible!' Liz said.

'I didn't get much sleep.'

'Well, perhaps you should go back home and get some,' Liz said rubbing my arm. 'Wait, you've had another dream, haven't you?'

Bowing my head, I said with dismay, 'Liz, it was you.'

'It was me?'

'You were in this convenience store and your face; it was the most awful look I have ever seen. There were tears in your eyes and you looked as if you were in pain.'

Our eyes met. Liz was speechless. I pleaded with her, 'Don't go into an express or a corner shop of any kind. If you need a few items, go to the supermarket regardless of the inconvenience. Something bad will happen to you if you do...'

My hand was shaking. I reached into my jacket for my lighter and cigarettes. Finding my lighter but no cigarettes, I realised that I had already smoked my last one. Turning to my sister, I said, 'Get a seat in the café. I'll meet you there in a minute.'

I rushed off down the street to find a shop with cigarettes. I was so caught up with getting cigarettes that I didn't hear my sister shout after me. I ran into the first shop that I came to.

I got to a few feet in front of the counter before I took note of my surroundings. A young man with a pistol was pointing it at the shop assistant behind the till. I stood motionless and silent, not wanting to alarm the robber. It was during that moment of silence that I became aware of the accomplice I had walked straight past on entering the store.

Suddenly, the bell above the door rang as another unsuspecting customer entered the store. I heard the new customer say, 'Ron,' and realised that it was my sister. I noted Liz's stunned appearance. It was then that I looked at the man stood between us.

The hooded rogue was huge and very agitated. I could see that he was unsettled by first me and then my sister coming into the shop.

He walked over to my sister and took hold of her handbag. He said, pushing Liz aside, 'I'll have that!'

Without thinking, I grabbed hold of him and shoved him into a display of reduced-price coffee. He stumbled, knocking three jars to the floor. One of the jars smashed. Then there was a loud bang. The shop became silent.

I looked to my sister. She was just as I had dreamt the night before. Her face was a picture of horror, pain and sadness. She didn't speak a word as tears streamed from her eyes. She still held her handbag. I felt a warm pain in the middle of my chest.

I felt my chest with my hand and looked down at my fingers. They were soaked with blood. The bullet had passed straight through me; blood poured from the wound. I looked up at Liz in shock, I saw her mouth the words 'I love you' as the bag I'd been carrying dropped from my hand. I watched Mum's gift-wrapped tin roll to my sister's feet, before the room became consumed in darkness.

Fate or Destiny

Her name was Tracy Ellis. In primary school she and I were opposites. She was attractive and popular; I was a geek and dressed to suit. Back then she hated me. She would never speak, except to tease me and if I smiled she would turn her head. In spite of this, she still had a place in my heart.

My feelings for her grew on moving up to high school. Socially, we were miles apart, but maturity had enabled us to talk. She sat beside me and often we would be paired together. She was so pretty and she smelt wonderful. She was a cheerleader and her obligations after school didn't give her much time to study. I would do her homework and on gaining an A she would say, 'Danny you're the best.' It would melt my heart.

One day, I psyched myself up to ask her out. I said, 'Tracy can I ask you something?' But when she faced me I lost my nerve and altered my question. Two weeks later, I saw her in the hall with her back to me. It was the perfect opportunity. I walked up behind her and poured out my feelings.

'Don't turn around. If you do, I won't be able to say this. I think you're wonderful. I love everything about you. I wake up every morning looking forward to school just so I can see you and at night you inhabit my dreams. You're in my heart and my mind. Please say yes when I ask, will you go out with me?'

And then she turned around. It was someone else. She smiled, hugged me and said, 'Yes!'

It wasn't to be the last time she would say yes. And that is how I met my wife.

Fear of the Dark

The room was dark, silent and still. I clung to my teddy, Sammy, so tight he could hardly breathe. Sammy didn't complain because he was scared too. We felt safer with each other and the nightlight beside the bed. The door was ajar. Mummy says there is no such thing as monsters and I tried to convince Sammy, but he was having none of it. Who was I fooling? They're real enough on TV.

'Don't worry, Sammy. I'll take care of you,' I said, kissing him on the head.

I stroked Sammy's fur repeatedly to try and get him to sleep, but his eyes remained fixed on the gap in the door, just like mine. The light peering from the hall was eerie and the silence haunting. Strange things happen at night; at least that's what Sammy told me.

A sudden low noise grabbed my attention. A muffled scratching, I could just hear it. It was coming from downstairs and I prayed that it would remain downstairs. No such luck. Soon the scratching sound was coming up the stairs, making its way up to the landing.

It crept along the carpeted hall and towards my door. I could not see what it was, but I would soon find out.

I shuddered in bed and pulled the covers up to my nose. Sammy pressed himself ever closer to my chest. I called out to my mum in a whisper, 'Mum. Mum,' but she couldn't hear me. I noticed the gap in the door getting bigger as the scratching ceased and something began to come in.

The door creaked open. The light from the hall cast a beam across the covers of my bed, highlighting me. I saw a shadow in the doorway.

I shut my eyes and squeezed them together as tight as I could. I didn't want to see it and I told myself that if I couldn't see it, it wouldn't see me. If only I could close my ears. It was in the room and moving about at the foot end of the bed.

Suddenly, it leapt onto the covers. I screamed and screamed, 'Mummy! Mummy!' The prowler scampered off my bed as quickly as it had leapt on and raced down the stairs.

A few seconds later and I was sitting up and resting in my mother's arms. Though I was crying, I was comforted by her presence.

'There, there, now. There's nothing to worry about. It was only the cat. I'm here,' Mum said, kissing my head.

'Can Sammy have a kiss too?' I asked.

'Of course he can,' Mum said, leaning over to Sammy. She tucked us back into bed before kissing me on the head once more.

I saw Dad in the doorway. He too had come when I called. As Mum joined him at the far end of my room, she turned and said, 'Goodnight, Martin. I love you.'

'I love you too, Mummy,' I replied, feeling much better.

'I know,' she said, before closing the door and leaving a small gap, 'sweet dreams.'

Finding A Way Forward

'Roy Pizer, how nice to see you,' a familiar voice said. I turned from the shop counter to find Amy, a girl I used to work with. I hadn't seen her in a couple of years.

'Oh hi, how are you?'

'Good and you?'

'Not bad. Uh, you still working at the office?'

'Yes, and with the same people. Nothing much changes.'

Nothing changes? Don't I wish that was the case? If only she knew. In normal circumstances I'd be thrilled to see her, but today I felt uncomfortable and wanted to get away. I knew it wouldn't be that easy. Amy and I were close once and could talk about anything. I knew she would still see me in that way, but I had no desire to rekindle past affection.

'Well, give my best to the others when you see them,' I said, edging towards the door.

'Will do. Are you still working for that company you went to work for?'

'Uh, no.'

'Oh? Where are you working now?'

'I'm not.'

'Oh, that's too bad. Hey, why don't I talk to Richard? I'm sure I can persuade him to give you your old job back.'

'No, it's not quite that easy. Valerie died last year. My job is looking after the kids.'

Amy's jaw dropped. She looked shocked and lost for words. She stammered, 'Oh, I'm so sorry, Roy.'

'It's OK. You weren't to know.' Funny how you lose contact so quickly when you move from one job to another.

'Where are the boys now, at school?'

'Yes, I fetch them at three.'

'Well, what are you doing now?'

'I look after our home, I guess.'

'Why don't we get a coffee across the road?' Amy asked.

'Uh, sure.' I didn't want to, but I couldn't say no. I'd never turned her down before and to do so now would make her even more uncomfortable. She just wanted to help and I didn't want to sour memories for the sake of half an hour.

Sitting across from each other in the empty coffee shop, Amy sipped her latte and smiled. Even now, after such a long time, we could share a moment of companionable silence. She knew me well. For eight years we worked alongside one another. We used to have a laugh and joke about and even flirt occasionally. We were the best of friends, but that was it, just friends. Yes, I found her attractive and I'm sure if I'd been single, I'd have asked her out, but I wasn't and I never cheated on Valerie.

'So, how old are the boys now?' Amy asked setting down her cup.

'Callum's eight and Michael's six.'

'God, it only seems like yesterday when you told me your wife was expecting. Oh, sorry,' she said, as I dipped my head.

'It's OK.'

'How are they?'

'Better than they were ten months ago. Michael still cries before bed.'

Both of us went quiet. This time the silence seemed awkward. She bit her lip and her coffee cup shook slightly.

'Say, have you met anyone yet? What was that guy's name that you went out with from the warehouse?' I asked, taking a sip from my own cup.

'Ethan, and, like everyone else, it didn't work out,' she replied with a giggle and shrugged.

'Why not?' I was always intrigued that she was on her own, such an attractive woman.

'Turns out that he was one of those sci-fi nuts who had trouble getting to grips with reality.'

'What do you mean? He was obsessed with watching reruns of The X-Files?'

'More like fixated with Star Trek. You know, he actually asked me if I would dress up like a Klingon in the bedroom.'

I burst out laughing. It was the first time I had laughed in over a year. I felt more at ease now and she too was smiling.

'This is great. I'm so glad I bumped into you. Say, why aren't you at work?'

'I booked the morning off to get a few things done. Don't have to be there for another hour yet. I'm glad we met too,' she said. Then she placed her hand on mine.

I shot up from the table.

'Sorry, I'm sorry,' I said, 'I didn't mean to react that way.' I sat back down feeling rather stupid.

'It's OK, Roy.'

'No, I'm sorry.'

'It's OK. You've been through such a lot.'

'No, I'd better go,' I said standing up. Fumbling about my pockets, I produced a handful of change to pay for our drinks. 'Thanks for the coffee. It was wonderful to see you.'

'It's alright, Roy. I got it.'

'Thanks. Uh, goodbye.' I raced out of the shop.

My head was a muddle. I walked straight past the road I needed to get back home. Amy had done nothing wrong and yet it felt as though she were making a pass. And what if she was? Where's the harm in that? Valerie's dead, but it still seemed like I was being unfaithful. Why can't I move on?

I came across an open park and took a seat on a bench. There was no one around, just me and the noise of the wind. It was then that I cried, harder than I had ever before. It was an uncontrollable sobbing that sent a shiver throughout my body.

'Are you alright?' a voice asked in front of me. With teary eyes I looked up to see a woman in a white dress.

'I will be. Just need a minute or two.'

'Here take this,' she said, handing me a handkerchief.

'Thanks,' I replied.

'It's good to find somewhere you can collect your thoughts,' she said, as I tried to calm down. 'I come here to remember loved ones. It's a place where you can reflect and gain strength. It takes time to find a way forward. You'll find your way and, like me, you'll come to accept change and become a better person for it.'

'Thank you,' I said, lifting my head, but she was gone. It was as though she had never been; had I imagined her? Then I remembered the handkerchief. I looked at it and noted the letters 'VP' embroidered on it. Valerie? Impossible. Was it coincidence or did I have it in my pocket all along? I didn't know, but I was sure of what I had to do next and I knew exactly where she would be.

Like Mother, Like Daughter

All I want is for Mum to be happy. Every day, between household chores, she sits at the kitchen table looking over other people's photos and status updates on social networking sites. If she's not doing that, she's playing some kind of pointless online game. She's depressed and I wish there was a way I could help her.

She doesn't have any real friends and she never goes out. She only socializes with work colleagues and her job is during school hours for a couple of days a week. She could do with a real job, something better than being stuck behind the till of the estate supermarket. She's so much better than that, if only she would believe it.

Mum's lonely. Ever since she and Dad got divorced, there's never really been anyone in her life. She's had plenty of dates, all of which ended as quickly as they started, and it isn't because of a lack of sex, as she has had the occasional one night stand. Mum's just not ever met the right guy and I'm sure she thinks she never will.

I've only recently been able to understand her loneliness, now that I have met Jay. Jay's wonderful. He's not like other guys. He's not afraid to tell me that he loves me; he's not embarrassed to hold my hand. We can talk for hours about anything and he drives me home from school whenever he is not at work. Mum doesn't like him, but I think that's because she's jealous.

'Off out with Jay tonight?' Mum asked as I was putting on my shoes.

'Yeah, that's right,' I answered, without looking at her.

She lit a fag and asked, 'Where's he taking you?'

'Bowling, I think?'

'Have a good night. See you at eleven,' Mum said, just as I opened the door.

Turning around to face her, I said, 'You don't have to wait up, Mum. I'll be fine. Why don't you get yourself an early night?'

'The sooner you get home, the sooner I'll get to sleep.'

'Mum, I'm sixteen. I'm not a child anymore. I'm old enough to look after myself.'

'You might be sixteen, but you're not an adult. I know what this is about.'

'Know what?'

'I'm not stupid, Holly. I was sixteen once and I know it doesn't take four hours to bowl.'

'And why shouldn't we? We have been going out for three weeks now and we love each other. It's not like it's illegal.'

'Because you are too young and you still live in this house! I could care less about what the law says. You're not going out and that's final.'

I couldn't look at her and I'd be damned if I was going to stay in just because she didn't want me to go out with Jay. Gritting my teeth, I said, 'Remind me again how old you were when you had me.'

'Yes, and that was a mistake.'

That was it. I walked out.

'Holly, wait!' Mum yelled after me. 'Holly, I didn't mean it! I'm sorry! Holly!'

I didn't turn around. I got into the passenger seat of Jay's car at the end of the drive. 'Bitch,' I said, as we sped off, but I didn't say another word between the time we left my house and the time we arrived at a friend's house for the party.

It was one thirty when I eventually got in. On opening the front door, I was greeted by the overpowering stench of cigarette smoke.

Mum came into the hall from the kitchen. 'And what time do you call this? … Oh my god! What happened to you?'

Before getting home, I had been hoping that Mum had gone to bed, even though I knew she wouldn't. The bruise under my left eye must have been worse than I thought for Mum to notice from where she was standing.

'Come here. Let me have a look at that.'

'Can't I just go to bed?' I pleaded, before walking over to her.

Pulling a chair out from the table, Mum said, 'Take a seat while I get some ice from the freezer.'

As I held a bag of frozen peas to my eye, Mum asked, 'Did, Jay do this?'

Hanging my head, I made a string of excuses, 'He didn't mean it. He loves me really. He was drunk and…'

'And these are the same sort of things I used to say to your grandmother about your father,' Mum said, taking the bag away from my eye. 'Why did Jay hit you?'

'Because I said I didn't want to do it,' I replied. 'After our argument, I didn't feel up to it. He called me a tease.'

'Come here,' Mum said, resting my head on her chest. She too was crying, but somehow I sensed that she was proud of me. 'It took years and a whole lot of bruises before I was strong enough to kick your dad into touch. I don't want to see you go through the same thing I did. He's not worth it.'

Mum and I talked until close to three in the morning, a real heart to heart. We laughed, we cried and, despite the swollen eye, somehow I felt better.

Late the next morning, Mum decided that she had to go grocery shopping. In spite of my protest, she dragged me with her. Sitting in the passenger seat of Mum's hatchback, I felt like a prize idiot, wearing dark sunglasses when it wasn't even sunny. Gazing out the window, I saw the super-mart on the left, but Mum had driven straight over the roundabout.

'Mum, the super-mart was that way,' I said, turning towards her.

'It's alright, I've got a few errands on the other side of town to do first,' Mum replied, keeping her focus on the road.

Ten minutes later, we pulled into the parking lot of Pete's Auto and Tyres. I looked at her quivering in disbelief.

'Mum, what are you doing? This is where Jay works.'

'I know,' Mum said, reversing into a spot next to Jay's car. 'I'm going to have a word with him.'

'Please, Mum! Let's just go, like now!'

'Calm down, Holly. It'll just be a quiet word.'

'No, Mum, please! Mum!'

Crunch! Mum had backed straight into Jay's car. The sound of the metal buckling back out made me wince as Mum eased the car forward.

'Shit,' Mum said, then looked over to me. I didn't say a word.

Mum got out of the car just as Jay and two other men in overalls came out from the garage to have a look. Standing with his mouth wide open, Jay was silent and still as he realised that the car was his. Then he looked at me. I turned my head in shame, just as I had felt when he stood over me the night before.

'I'm really sorry. I wasn't paying attention,' Mum said to Jay as he walked over to his car. As he knelt down to inspect the damage, Mum leaned in towards him. She no longer had an apologetic look on her face.

'Touch my daughter again and you'll have more than a dent in your car to worry about.'

We got back in the car and drove off, leaving Jay to think on what had just happened.

'Holly, why don't we forget about the shopping and get something to eat instead? What do you think?' Mum said, as we rejoined the traffic on the main road.

'I'd like that,' I replied, taking my glasses off. Smiling, I thought, Mum might not have a man in her life, but she will never be lonely. She will always have me.

Locked In

Driving down a back road, I could make out the hunched figure of a hitchhiker in the rain. Pulling up beside him, I rolled down the window and asked, 'Need a lift?'

He nodded.

'Hop in.'

His jacket and clothes were soaked through. He must have been out in the rain for some time. He coughed and sneezed and then folded his arms together in an attempt to get warm. He looked to be in his early to mid-twenties, but I couldn't make out much more of his appearance. His face was covered by the hood of the jumper he wore under his denim coat.

'Where are you heading?'

'Just, out of town,' he replied, wiping a bead of water from the end of his nose.

'Where would you like me to drop you off, at the next village we come to or in the city where I'm heading?'

'The city will do,' he said, unbuttoning his jacket. He wasn't the most talkative of fellows and he didn't attempt to continue with the conversation. After a while he broke the silence, 'Do you mind if I smoke? I couldn't roll one in the rain.'

'No, go ahead,' I replied. 'You wouldn't mind rolling me one of those, would you?'

'No, not at all,' he said, taking a small tin out from his inside pocket. He handed me a rollup, took down his hood and introduced himself.

'Josh,' he said.

'Ron.'

'Can I change the tunes, Ron?' he asked, putting his tobacco tin back into his jacket pocket.

'No, carry on,' I said, accepting a light.

'That'll do,' he said, as he leant back in his seat.

'Classic rock, I'd have thought that you would've picked something more modern.'

'Zeppelin, Floyd, anything from the seventies so long as it's not disco.'

The song on the radio was typical of the station and at least ten years older than the hitcher I'd picked up. For him it must have been just a song, but for me it was my childhood. Not the happiest time of my life, but it brought back memories of walking home from school and singing it at the top of my lungs. A magical moment, and for a few seconds I was back with my old crew. The daydream ended when the news cut in.

'Good evening, this is Mike Rogers with your CJKH FM news update. News on the hour, every hour. The time is eleven o'clock.

'Police have found the body of a girl in a field behind a multi-story car par. This is the fourth such killing in the area in three months. The hunt for the murderer continues and the police are asking for anyone with information to please come forward.

'Fire services have said that the burning of Dalton Springs Mall may have been arson. Police are holding two men for questioning in relation to the fire.

'And in sport, the Jays have beaten the Knights in the championship quarterfinals. It is the first time the Jays have advanced to the semis in seventeen years.

'This has been Mike Rogers with your CJKH FM news update and now back to Jack Simms for more classic hits before midnight.'

The music came back on as I stopped for some traffic lights. Pulling up beside a stationary police car, I signalled right in preparation to head south for the freeway. I glanced at Josh, who had slouched down in his seat. As the lights changed, the police carried on east. Josh sat up a few seconds later. I caught his gaze and raised an eyebrow, but said nothing.

I drove steadily along the single lane road. There was no traffic. Conversation from Josh had dried up. The only light came from the reflection of catseyes in the road, and the only thing to disrupt the monotony was the music on the stereo.

Josh was deep in thought and I wondered what was on his mind. I was about to ask, when I spotted a car coming up fast in my rear-view mirror.

'Looks as though our friends have returned,' I said, shaking my head.

'Shit,' Josh replied, gazing into the wing mirror, 'what are they doing?'

'Just following us, by the looks of it.'

'Do you think they're going to pull us over?' Josh asked. His voice trembled.

'Yeah.'

'What are you going to do?'

'I'm going to turn down this side road and see if they follow.'

Sure enough, as I signalled left so did the police car tailing us. My young passenger was beginning to panic and though I was maintaining a calm appearance, inside I was shaking.

'They're still behind us!' Josh exclaimed.

'Shut up, would you!' I snapped. 'Trust me to pick up someone the police are looking for.'

'Sorry, man, but…'

'But, shut the fuck up, unless you want to join that slut I've got in the boot!'

Josh pressed himself up against the door and I could sense the fear in his eyes. I could also see that he was thinking of jumping out of the car, but we were moving too fast. I couldn't care less if he did. I was only interested in how I was going to lose my tail before more of the boys in blue arrived.

'What's that up ahead?' Josh asked, pointing at something up the way. It was a road block and soon the flashing lights reappeared in my mirror.

I put my foot down and raced towards the barriers. Turning his head towards me, Josh asked, 'What are you doing?'

'They're not taking me alive.'

Seventy, eighty, ninety, soon we were doing more than a hundred. We were outpacing the tailing squad car, but the blockade in front of us was drawing nearer.

'Don't be stupid, Ron. You'll never get through that.'

One ten.

'Think about it. It's not worth it.'

One fifteen.

'Slow down, man!'

One twenty.

'Hit the brakes!'

Suddenly, Josh unbuckled his seatbelt and pounced on me in an attempt to take the wheel. Fighting for control of the car, we veered off the road. The hollow must have been six feet deep, but the bank between the road and the ravine was three. I don't remember anything once we hit the ditch. I only remember seeing the wall of the embankment a second before all went black.

Three days later, I woke up in hospital. I felt nothing and could only move my eyes. From where I lay I couldn't see much, just the whitewashed ceiling and the bedside cabinet to the right of me.

I don't know what happened to Josh. I snapped my spine in the crash and for now I'm dependent on twenty-four-hour care. I may not have died and I may not spend the rest of my days in prison, but it would seem that God had another punishment in mind. No one gets better from this. The surgeons may tidy up my face, but I'll never talk again. Without the machine and the tube in my throat, I wouldn't be able to breath. I'm lucky they even know I'm alive.

I suppose some of you will think that I got what I deserve, a life sentence of solitude and suffering. However, for those of you who are compassionate, you may think my sentence harsh and may even have sympathy. Don't. A leopard doesn't change its spots and my mind is as active as ever. I pray every day for someone to end this miserable existence, but in the meantime it's my thoughts that maintain my sanity. I take the greatest pleasure from the five victims I picked up, whose innocence I stole, souls I tortured and bodies I violated. I won't be the only one to suffer. Unlike them I have no one to leave behind, but my legacy will haunt their families until their dying days and that brings a smile to my face. I can still do that.

No Regrets

Where am I? What time is it? I leant up and was immediately aware of the pounding in my head.

I looked to my right. No clock. Of course not, it's not my house. Who's house is this? How did I get here? The ache in my head convinced me to stay put.

I scrambled my hand along the bedside table and found my watch. 4:20am, shit.

I slipped my watch on. I heard a groan to my left. I looked over and discovered a naked woman beside me. I smiled. Got to do something about this head.

I got out of bed as quietly as I could and snuck out of the room. The bathroom was directly opposite. I closed the door and turned on the lights. Man, that's bright. I opened the medicine cabinet and to my relief there was plenty of paracetamol. After taking two tablets I drank from the tap. Never had water tasted so good.

I turned the tap off and looked in the mirror. My bloodshot eyes gazed back at me. The water helped, but a few more hours of sleep wouldn't go amiss. Do I slip back in bed? No, I need to get home. At least there I won't get disturbed. Who was that girl? I didn't recognise her. Should I leave a note? No, I'll get dressed and see myself out. It's probably for the best.

I turned off the light, snuck back in the bedroom and quietly picked my clothes off the floor. After pulling my jeans on, I walked to the bedside table to retrieve my wallet. I looked inside. Not a single note.

I looked at the girl on the bed and smiled again. Since breaking up with my ex, Julie, sex had been hard to come by. Unfortunately, I couldn't remember it. Still, I'm sure I must have enjoyed it.

She rolled over and I admired her breasts. What a set. She brushed her hair from her face. Fuck! It is my ex! What have I done?

Suddenly, the recollection of the whole night came flooding back; the quick drink after work, bumping into an old friend, following him to a club, and the party. It was there that I ran into Julie. She was drunk and began to crack on to me. Then I remembered something I said.

'Julie, if the continuation of the human race depended on the two of us, I'd let mankind go extinct.'

Why didn't I just leave when I saw her? Why did I have to keep drinking? Whatever possessed me to get back into bed with this woman I despise? I sure hope I wore protection. I can't see anything about. What if she's given me a disease or worse, she comes to me telling me she's pregnant? You fucking idiot, how do you keep getting into this kind of mess? I got to go.

I marched out of the bedroom and down the hall. The corridor opened into an immense lounge. There were bodies and empty cans strewn about the floor. I made my way to the front door through a minefield of debris.

Leaning against the door was the largest man I had ever seen. He had sick all down his shirt and someone had put make-up on his face. I tried to shift him, but quickly realised it was no use. Everyone else was in a similar state. There was no other way out of the apartment. I'd have to wait until morning.

Maybe I deserve this. Maybe if I wasn't such an idiot my whole life, then I wouldn't find myself in this predicament. Maybe if I had paid Julie more attention, we wouldn't have split up. This is my fault. I'm useless.

No, I'm talking shit. I need sleep. Maybe I'll just crash in here. I don't want to crash in here. Fuck, back into bed with Julie.

When I got back to the bedroom, Julie was still asleep. I opened the wardrobe. It creaked loudly. I winced and pulled out a spare duvet and spread it out on the floor.

'You don't have to do that, Jim. You can come back to bed if you like,' Julie said unmoving.

'No, it's fine. I can't. It's one thing to sleep with you when I'm out of my head, it's another to do so sober,' I replied digging out a spare pillow.

'We didn't do anything,' she said as she sat up. 'You were already passed out, when I climbed in with you. And I certainly wasn't going to sleep with you after what you said to me.'

'Then, why..?'

'I was too drunk to get home on my own and I didn't feel safe out there. Some huge guy was trying it on with me, before he got sick on me and himself. I had nowhere else to go. I know you hate me, but surely you don't hate me that much.'

'I don't hate you,' I replied, sitting down on the corner of the bed. 'It takes two to tango and maybe I'm as much to blame.'

'It wasn't you who cheated.'

'No, you've got that right. Have you any idea how much that hurt?'

'Yes I do.'

'Like fuck.'

'Yes I do. I still love you and know I can never get you back. I wish I could erase what happened, but I can't. I've got to live with it and it's sure to haunt me for a very long time,' Julie said and started to cry.

'I shouldn't have said what I said. I'm sorry,' I said climbing back into bed. I pulled her towards me and cuddled her. 'You're right, we're never going to get back together, but we don't have to go on as enemies. I still care about you and I'd like to think that one day you'll find someone and be happy.'

'Thanks, Jim,' she replied as I kissed her on the head.

'If it makes you feel any better, I wouldn't let the world go extinct.' I smiled and she giggled. 'Goodnight, Julie.'

'Goodnight, Jim.'

No Strings Attached

'JUST A SIMPLE CALL Attractive, active female, 36, blue eyes, seeks like-minded, attractive male, for afternoon of fun, no strings attached.'

That's what the ad on the website said. Just a simple call and no strings attached. Perfect.

I picked up the phone and began to dial the local number. I got to the fifth digit and ended the call. An overwhelming sense of anxiety suddenly overtook me. God, do I know what I'm doing? Pull yourself together. I took a deep breath and then punched in all six numbers on my cordless.

Three ring tones and every one of them seemed agonisingly long before a sweet and enticing voice answered the call.

'Hello?'

Her voice was gentle, kindly and strangely seductive but none of that eased my rising nerves. With a slight tremble in my voice I replied, 'Hi, I'm calling in regards to the ad on your web space.'

'How nice, I was just thinking I could do with a little company,' she replied. 'My name's Debra, what's yours?'

'David…Dave is fine.'

'Well, Dave, where do you live?'

'Uh…about a mile north of town.'

'I live on the other side of the river, 15 Massey Road. I'm not doing anything at the moment. Would you like to come round, say in an hour?'

'Sure.'

'My house is the one with the gate and the red door.'

'Great. I look forward to meeting you. I'll see you in an hour then. Is there anything you would like me to bring?'

'No, just yourself. See you in an hour.'

After the phone went dead I felt as giddy as a teenager having secured a date for the prom. My nervous tension had gone and I was floating on air.

As I pulled up at the kerb outside Debra's house, my nervousness returned. The house itself was not unlike my own. It was a semi and it appeared to have at least two bedrooms. The curtains were drawn and before me there was a wall with a black steel gate and short stone path leading up to a red door.

Opening the glove box of my silver saloon, I slipped my wedding ring from my finger and placed it on the upper shelf. I took my wallet out from the back pocket of my trousers and opened it to retrieve the condom I had hidden inside. If the wedding ring was a stark reminder of the guilt pervading me, then the family portrait of my wife and two kids was positively austere. I stuffed the condom into my trouser pocket and tossed my wallet into the glove box before stepping out from the car.

The street was quiet with very few cars about. I could see but one other parked a few houses further up. I opened the gate. It creaked noisily, making me jump, and my hands shook as I closed it.

The path was short and although my mind was full of thoughts of turning back and making a quick getaway, somehow my feet had carried me to the single step, confronted by a polished brass knocker. I gave it three sharp knocks.

Like my initial phone call, the brief delay before the door opened seemed unbelievably long. However, my fears were eased on meeting my host. Debra was stunningly beautiful. She stood in the open doorway and leaned provocatively against its frame. She had vivid red hair and a curvaceous figure and though she was edging towards middle age, she looked at least ten years younger and had an accentuated confidence that was so very alluring.

'Come in,' she invited, with a short flutter of her eyelashes.

I smiled and said nothing before following her down a hallway into her fashionable lounge. The room was calming, with plenty of subdued lighting, well placed floral arrangements and luxurious furnishings that worked well to soften the mood. It had the feminine touch that is most evident in a childfree home.

'Please, take a seat. Would you like a drink? A glass of wine, coffee, tea, perhaps?'

'Tea would be great.' I perched on the edge of her couch as she slipped into the adjoining kitchen.

She returned with a dainty cup on a matching saucer. She sat down across from me in the single seater, with one leg over the other, exposing its shapely suppleness. Placing her own cup and saucer down upon the modern glass table between us, she asked, 'What do you do for a living, Dave?'

'I'm a Design Engineer for a company in the city,' I answered coolly, taking a sip from my cup before setting it down on the table.

'How long have you been married?'

How did she know? I looked down at my ring finger and noticed the smooth indent left by the gold band I had never previously removed since my wedding day. With a false show of confidence, I answered truthfully, 'Seven years.'

'Don't look so worried. No strings attached remember. I'm going upstairs to slip into something more comfortable. Finish your tea and I'll see you in a moment.'

She stood up and sauntered slowly towards me, casually running her fingers through my hair as she passed. It would have been one of the most sensual moments of my life had my heart not been pounding with trepidation. I looked back and saw her standing at the base of the stairs. She paused for a moment and, after giving me a wink and a seductive smile, went up.

I know I didn't run, but I can't remember walking to the front door or making it to the gate at the end of the path. The ominous creak made me wince as I tried to squeeze through as small a gap as possible. Fumbling to get my keys into the car door, I suddenly became aware of someone standing beside me.

'Dave? Is that you?'

I glanced over my shoulder. One of my neighbours was carrying two shopping bags from the express at the far end of the street. I shoved my naked hand into my pocket.

'Nancy, how nice to see you.'

'Just been to the shop for my mum. What brings you to this side of the river?'

'Just dropping off some documents for a colleague during my lunch break. Sorry, must dash.'

The narrow lane was only just wide enough to make a three point turn from a standing start, but as I was in such a rush I simply hopped the kerb. I never looked back in the mirror to gauge the reaction of my startled neighbour, nor did I look out the window to see if Debra had seen me leave. Before I knew it, I was signalling left towards the dual carriageway for the north end of town.

Fifteen minutes later, I pulled up outside my house. Turning off the ignition, I reached into the glove box and retrieved my wallet. I slipped my wedding ring back onto my finger and smiled. Perhaps it was for the best.

Walking into my house and into the front room, I was unexpectedly greeted by my wife. She was still dressed in her uniform and had yet to remove the pens or the fob watch from her top pocket.

'Lynn, this is a nice surprise. What are you doing home?' I asked, fearing the worst.

'This afternoon's surgery was cancelled, so they sent us home,' she replied, with a warm smile. She hugged me and whispered in my ear. It may have been awhile, but some things are certainly worth waiting for.

Repressed Milestones

'Good morning, you're through to the CJKH FM Morning Show, and who's our caller?' DJ Jack Simms asked.

'Brendan George.' I replied.

'Hi, Brendan, now are you ready to play 'You Pick The Decade'?'

'Yes I am, Jack.'

'Great, now let me explain the rules. I'm going to play you a few lines from a song from a decade of your choice and if you can tell me the name of the artist and the year of the song, I'll give you £100. Get three answers right and you qualify for the all or nothing prize. It is then that you must make a choice. You can either walk away with £300 or gamble it all for £1000. Are you ready, Brendan?'

'Yes.'

'What decade would you like?'

'The nineties, Jack.'

'Alright, here's the first song,' Jack said, as the first few notes came on the radio, 'Name the artist and tell me—'

'Bryan Adams, 1991.'

'Boy, that didn't take long.'

'I met my girlfriend that summer and it was number one for like forever.'

'Yes, sixteen weeks in fact. Well done, Brendan. Ready for the next one?'

'Yes.'

'Okay, same again. Name the—'

'Blur, 1995.'

'Correct. Again that was rather quick; how did you know that one so fast, Brendan?'

'I proposed to my girlfriend the week that song was released. She said yes.'

'Oh, wow. How very heart-warming. Brendan, all of a sudden, there are a few teary-eyed people here in the studio. Fantastic. Here's the next song. Who sung—'

'No Doubt, 1996.'

'That's right. Well, as usual, there was certainly no doubt in your mind with that answer.'

'It was number one around the time my girlfriend and I got married.'

'How wonderful.'

'We're not married anymore. We got divorced in 2001.'

'Oh, I'm sorry, but something tells me this just might be your lucky day, all the same. However, I don't want to sway your decision and I must remind you that you currently have £300. Now, it's your choice, you can either keep what you've won up to now and walk away or gamble for our top prize at the risk of losing it all. Brendan, what will it be?'

'I'm going to gamble, Jack.'

'Excellent. I sure hope you get it. Are you ready for the final question?'

'Yes, I am.'

'Okay, for £1000 name the artist and tell me the year.'

My mind went blank. It was an upbeat dance-pop song with a heavy reliance on the use of synthesizers and auto-tune. The voice of the singer was very familiar. Her tone was melodic, but mature. I was sure it was someone better known from a bygone era. I was becoming increasingly anxious and frustrated by my inability to recall both the name of the singer and the year of a song I should so easily know.

'Okay, Brendan, put us out of our misery. Who's the artist and what is the year of this classic song?'

'At a guess, I would say it sounds a bit like Cher, but I can't recall a single song she sung after eighty-nine.'

'It is Cher and this was her biggest solo hit.'

'It sounds too modern to have been in the early part of the nineties. Why can't I remember? I should know this.'

'Okay, Brendan, I need an answer. What is the year of the song?'

'1999?'

'Oh, I'm so sorry, Brendan. I'm afraid that's incorrect. It was a year earlier, 1998.'

The last two digits echoed in my mind, reverberating like a migraine that couldn't be ignored. I could no longer hear

Jack Simms' voice on the other end of the phone. I'd drifted into a flashback that I'd put out of my head from all those years ago.

'It's a wet and windy one again this morning,' the DJ said over the radio in my car. 'Unfortunately, it doesn't look like it's going to get any better over the next few days, but here's something that might add a little sunshine to your day. It's a new song from Cher. It's called "Believe" and it's sure to be the next number one.'

Tapping my fingers on the steering wheel to the beat, I glanced down at the time on the dash, 7:35am. Not a lot of time between getting to work and my first stop.

Suddenly, the car swivelled about the road. I gripped the steering wheel and tried to regain control. It swayed in and out of the lane, getting dangerously close to the oncoming traffic. I hit the brakes. The car spun. I saw headlights flashing all around me. Just as I straightened out I saw the front grill of a lorry racing towards me. I pulled back into my own lane, but there wasn't enough time to avoid the collision at the rear of the car. I looked back in horror at my two-year-old son.

'Christopher!'

Retail Opportunities

It was in the last hour before closing when I spotted her. She looked like any other student from the university. She was young, attractive, trendy and had an air of innocence about her. But there was something not quite right and that's why I was watching her.

I've been the Head of Security for the last three years and it's my job to deal with anything that has to do with the store's losses. Shoplifters, label switchers, bad returns, and employees skimming from the till all come under my watch. It's up to me to deal with them. The company like to refer to it as 'Loss Control' but I prefer 'Loss Prevention'. Last year some light-fingered opportunist cost the store eight grand.

It's rather amusing to watch a shoplifter at work. They think they are so clever. They try all sorts of tactics, but what they don't seem to realise is that I've seen it all before. It's their behaviour that gives them away. Standing along the back wall, looking around for security cameras and picking items off the rack without ever looking at their sizes. These are just some of the ways in which I'm alerted to their presence and this girl was no different.

She was on her own and kept her eyes to the floor. Whenever she stopped to look at something, she would leave her bag at her feet rather than keeping it slung over her shoulder. She also seemed to spend a lot of time in the men's suits section of the store. You might think that she was just looking for something for her boyfriend, but she didn't look like the kind of girl to be going out with a business man.

I followed her, watching from a safe distance. There were two employees in the section, one behind the counter at the far end of the store and her colleague, sorting items in a section close by. A middle-aged man was browsing over a selection of ties, and a woman in her late twenties was sampling cologne in the gift section. What I found interesting about this suspicious student was when another middle-aged man entered the section; she quickly picked up her bag and moved elsewhere when he got too close.

However, in spite of her odd behaviour, I didn't see her remove anything from the shelves or place them in her bag. She must have had some skill as a magician because I have a very good eye for the tell-tale signs of a shoplifter and I couldn't see her put anything into her pockets. She even made her way towards the door in a suspicious fashion. For thirty minutes she had wandered about the aisles like she had all the time in the world, but all of a sudden she had to leave like she would miss the last bus.

I discreetly gave chase. As soon as she got to the doors I planned to confront her. I didn't normally act on a hunch, but I was sure she was guilty. Just as she put her hand on the door, she stopped and glanced back to the other end of the store. I was about to jump out from behind a rack of clothes when I noticed her give some sort of a nod. I turned and looked back to where she had signalled. I suddenly realised I'd been tricked. Damn, the girl sampling cologne! She was my true perpetrator and was heading for the door at the opposite end of the store. Once out the exit I knew I'd never catch her. I hurried to get to the other end of the shop. She spotted me, smiled, raised her middle finger and then legged it.

It must have been my lucky day. She collided with a pensioner's trolley and was still on the floor when I arrived to apprehend her. Once I was certain the old lady was fine, I took my underhanded consumer by the arm and escorted her to the security room.

She neither cried nor displayed any hint of remorse. She sat at the table looking completely disinterested, waiting for me to commence with the routine of her arrest.

'Empty the contents of your bag onto the table, please,' I asked her.

She opened the clasp on her bag and I sensed my eyes widen as she took out a series of items in excess of a thousand pounds. She'd managed to lift a digital camera, a smartphone, the latest tablet, a men's dress watch, designer perfume, all of which had been lifted in the past, but never in one haul. It was an impressive take and I tried my best to keep my composure when moving the interrogation forward.

'No purse. No ID,' I said, looking through her vacant holdall. 'What's your name?'

She remained tight-lipped and looked at the ceiling. I stood up and slammed my hands on the table. She immediately turned her attention towards me and her unapologetic gaze met with mine.

'Name?'

'Cindy,' she muttered.

'Speak up.'

'Cindy,' she replied.

'Cindy what?'

'Cindy Rella,' she answered with a self-righteous smile.

'Very funny. I wonder if the police will find it so amusing.'

'Whatever. Isn't that what you're going to do anyway?'

We sat in silence for a time. She looked about the room, never focusing on any one thing for more than a couple of seconds. I looked at the items on the table and then at the clock on the wall. Seven minutes until closing. I still had an hour of work to do and dealing with the authorities was bound to keep me for another hour on to that. Then there was the paperwork and the obligatory phone call to the manager, who'd already gone home for the day. I could offer her the punishment of a fine; it would be simpler, but she'd never pay it.

I leaned forward and glared at her with a feeling of deep resentment. If it weren't for a senior citizen and her trolley, she would have got away with the largest single haul in the store's history and I would have had the humiliating pleasure of informing the branch manager of my inexplicable failure.

She met with my stare and then raised her middle finger once again while maintaining her self-imposed silence. Suddenly, I had an idea. I thought about it for a minute then stood up and walked over to the door.

'Go. Get out of here.'

'What?' she replied, sitting up in her chair.

'I'm letting you go. Consider this to be your lucky day.'

I could see the confusion on her face, but she got up from her seat and joined me at the door. I took hold of her arm. She shrugged off my grasp.

'Just lead the way,' she said and then followed me out of the security office.

I escorted her to the store's back entrance and held the door for her. As she walked past me to the exit, I said, 'Don't ever come back, not ever.'

'I won't,' she replied and left.

Back in the security office, I collected my jacket and my bag from the locker and prepared to go home. There was just one last thing I had to do before I left. I picked up the phone from the desk and called the branch manager. I rang him every night before I left and he answered my call soon after dialling.

'Hi, Len, I've got some bad news. A young woman somehow managed to make off with a considerable amount of electronic goods and I was unable to stop her.'

I explained to him how the woman and her accomplice had deceived me. He told me not to worry about it and that we would discuss it again come morning. I then walked over to the table, put the tablet, camera and other items that had been stolen in my bag, switched off the lights and then headed home.

Sinister Justice

Opening my eyes, I saw what appeared to be a collage of newspaper clippings stuck to the ceiling. The words seemed all but a blur in the dim light about the room. My mind was in a haze and it took a few minutes to register my surroundings.

I tried to sit up and quickly discovered that I was unable. My arms were bound with handcuffs and outstretched on the wooden board beneath me. My legs were also restrained and the best I could manage was to bend my knees.

Where am I? Why am I here? Oh no, please!

'Help! Help! Somebody! Anybody! Help!' I yelled, writhing.

'No one can hear you, Mr. Wilson. No one at all,' a soft voice emerged from the shadows. There was someone sitting in the corner of the room beyond my feet. I couldn't make out her appearance, but I knew that my captor was female.

'No one could hear me and my sister when we were down here,' she said, as she stood up and walked towards me. 'Not even our mother, and she would be sitting in the living room but fifteen feet above your head.'

She stepped into the light to the right of me. Her hair was brown, fine and shoulder length. She was slender and casually dressed. She could hardly be much older than my eldest grandchild. She looked vaguely familiar. She neither smiled nor frowned, but the coldness of her eyes was most telling. They seemed pitiless and I was sure that she was not about to show me any kind of remorse. I was at her mercy and beneath my portly exterior I was trembling.

'Why me? I don't know you. Is it because I'm a man of God? Whatever sins you've committed, I'm sure we can walk the path to forgiveness together,' I said, with heavy breaths.

My callous host kept silent until I had finished my desperate plea. She gazed over my naked torso.

'You are here to repent your sins, and though you don't know me, I certainly know you. You are Father Alan Wilson, the vicar of St. Michael's church. My father was one of your disciples. He was an alcoholic and in his drink-fuelled rage he would beat my mother, but that was nothing compared to what he did to me and my sister.'

'You're one of Father Sandwell's daughters,' I replied. 'He died five years ago. Have you not gained salvation from his death?'

'How can someone gain salvation when their abuser never repented nor received punishment for their crimes? My father may have died from the drink, but he passed away peacefully after doing what he did best, shrouding his guilt in the depths of a bottle.

'He had a nice service, remember? You spoke of the good my father did for the community in the service of God. You also said that God would accept him into his kingdom and that my father would be forever a part of our lives. You got that right. I haven't been able to put him out of my mind and neither could my sister. That is, until she took her own life.

'Ironic, don't you think? My father was an abusive alcoholic and, according to your preaching, has been accepted into heaven and my sister has been refused because she opted for suicide. Where's the justice in that?

'Did you know that she was shunned by members of our faith and family because she desecrated her body with tattoos and piercings? She didn't like who she was. She couldn't accept the image she saw in the mirror. The problem is you can alter your appearance, but you can't change your memories. They haunt you forever and pain you like a splinter that can't be removed.'

'I'm sorry about what happened to you and your sister but I didn't know. I couldn't stop it. I'm not to blame.'

'Do not insult me by trying to mask your guilt with lies!' my captor exclaimed before quelling her anger. 'I've been honest with you and I would expect that you extend me the same courtesy. I've already extracted the truth from the others. All I expect from you is a confession.

'You know, I don't know which is worse: he who commits the crime or those who choose to hide it. At least with my father he was driven by his passion for his needs, in spite of how sick they were. You were only interested in saving the reputation of the institution, deliberately forsaking the very morals you preach. My sister and I were sacrificed to save face and hence our torture was prolonged.

'We were ignored by Miss Brayton when we came to her for help, and our father punished us severely after speaking to Reverend Woods. They and the others I've killed elected to protect the institution. But before they all died, they pointed the finger towards you, Father Wilson, patron saint for protecting abuse and paedophilia.

'Well, that's all in the past, and so to the present. Is there anything you'd like to say before we commence?'

I could see that it wouldn't matter what I might say. In spite of this, I attempted to make her see reason, while she secured a steel cord to a hook above my head.

'You won't get away with this. The police will find you and when they do, you'll get life.'

'I don't care. You're the last. After tonight I'll have completed my resolve and prison will be a welcome consequence.'

She checked to see if the cord was taught and then walked away. Though I was terrified when she was at my side, it was far worse not knowing where she was. The thought of what she was about to do made me pray for mercy.

I heard a metallic catch click on something mechanical. She was somewhere by my feet and the sound of a crank echoed about the room. Slowly, the head end of the platform where I lay began to lift.

'In spite of my sins and those who have sinned against me, I still have faith and wish to repent. My father's crimes were far worse than my own. He was penitent and was accepted into heaven, so I see no reason why I shouldn't,' she said, winding the crank. 'Forgive me, Father, for I have sinned. I have killed four people and soon a fifth. I know it is wrong to kill and that it goes against your Commandments, but they were all deserving given the crimes they committed.'

She then named each of her victims and secured the cable once I was vertical. Outstretched and helpless like Jesus on the cross, I could see the collage of news clippings clearly. The headlines were of each of the victims she had named, 'Parish Worker Missing', 'Civil Servant's Body Found in Estuary'.

My heart was pounding. I couldn't hear her confession as my mind was consumed with fear. She ceased to chant and retrieved an odd looking implement from a table along the far wall. It was long, curved and pointed. I prayed that it wouldn't go where I believed it was intended. A moment later she stood before me, examining her vicious tool with sinister affection.

'I want you to feel pain and indignity before you die,' she said, moving uncomfortably closer. 'Perhaps God will accept your pleas for forgiveness when you reach the gates of heaven, otherwise, see you in hell.'

She then began to recite the passage of my last rights. Sadly, I knew the rest.

Smitten

'Where is she?' my wife, Alison, asked before pushing her way into the room. 'Come out! I know you're in here, bitch!'

'Who you calling bitch, bitch!' Stephanie yelled, stepping out of the wardrobe. I grabbed hold of her arm to stop her from punching Alison.

'Come on then! Bring it on!' my wife taunted.

I put myself between them, stretching my arms out to keep them apart. I gestured for Alison to take a seat and then guided Stephanie to sit on the end of the bed. My head was a mess. What the fuck am I going to do? I may have quelled the situation, but this was sure to explode. I put my hands to my face as I stood in silence for the brief moment my two lovers allowed.

'Have you any idea what you're doing? He's a married man. What have you got to say for yourself?'

'That doesn't make you a good wife. Far from it, from what I hear.'

'Slut!' Alison yelled, leaping out of her chair. I moved in the way to stop her from attacking Steph.

'Yeah, well it's me he keeps coming back to. You obviously can't satisfy him under the sheets.'

I pushed Alison back into her chair. 'I'll kill you,' she said to Steph over my shoulder.

'Not if I get you first!' Steph replied.

'Can we please calm down? Please,' I asked, glancing between them before taking a seat next to Steph.

'Andrew, what are you doing?' Alison asked as she began to cry. 'You don't need her. I love you. We can work this out.'

'Alison, we've been over this. I don't love you. It's over,' I said, pulling Steph closer to me.

Steph snuggled in tight. I couldn't see her face, but I could tell by the reaction on Alison's that my lover was acting smug. Alison looked pale. Tears welled up in her eyes and in those few seconds she looked as though she aged ten years.

'You do know you weren't the first?' Alison blurted in an acidic tone. 'There have been others. My best friend, the woman across the road and his secretary, just to name a few.'

'Is this true?' Steph asked, suddenly shying away.

'Yeah... well...'

Steph stared up at me in disbelief. She was shaking and she turned her head from me when I met her gaze.

'They were before I met you. There's been no one else. I swear. Please don't cry. I love you, Steph. With all my heart.'

'Lies, all lies,' Alison said, rolling her eyes.

'Shut up,' I replied. I reached over to give Steph a hug, but she held out her hand in defiance. I turned to Alison, clenching my fists and grinding my teeth. 'Don't you think you've already caused me enough pain in the eleven years we've been married? This is why I want a divorce.'

'I think I'd better leave,' Steph said, as she stood up and walked towards the door.

'Steph, wait,' I called. She stopped halfway between the bed and the doorway. 'At least let me take you home.'

'No, I can see myself out,' she replied, continuing on her way.

'Yeah, see ya,' Alison said, with a self-satisfied smile.

Steph stopped once more and glared at Alison with searing eyes. I could sense her anger behind the tears she was holding back.

'Come on, how old are you, twenty-two, twenty-three?' Alison asked, as she stood up to watch Steph leave. 'Did you really think it would work? You're just another tart in the midst of Andy's midlife crisis.'

'No, you're wrong,' I said to Alison, who turned to face me. 'I was serious when I said I want a divorce. Please, Steph, don't leave. I love you.'

I held out my arms and, to my relief, Steph began to walk back towards me. Alison stepped in front of her. Before I could get to her, Alison said, 'You're nothing but a cheap slag and I'll always be around to stand in your way. He'll be mine again before you know it.'

Steph hit Alison with an almighty swing of her hand and my wife fell to the floor. I quickly jumped in and took hold of Steph by the shoulders, moving her aside before she had time to kick her while she was down. I turned and looked down at Alison. She lay on the carpet weeping and wheezing for breath. I knelt down to her. I'd never seen her look so white and helpless. I looked up at Steph.

'I'm sorry. I didn't mean to. She... oh, God.'

I stood up and rubbed Steph's shoulders. 'Look, everything will be alright. Go to the kitchen. Boil the kettle or something. I'll make sure she's OK and then we'll all talk this over.' I kissed her on the forehead and then went back to my wife on the floor.

Steph never got to the kitchen. I called her back just a few seconds later.

'Steph! Get the phone!' I yelled.

'What's the matter?' she asked, standing in the doorway.

'Call 999. She's stopped breathing.'

I turned Alison over and tilted her head back. I tried to resuscitate her. As I pushed firmly downwards on my wife's chest, I could hear the panic in Steph's voice as she spoke with the emergency services.

'Come on, Alison! Come on!' I shouted, before breathing into her mouth once more.

'An ambulance is on its way,' Steph said on re-entering the bedroom.

'She's not responding! Please, God, no!' I exclaimed, pushing down on the lifeless body before me. I briefly glanced up at Steph between compressions. 'She must have landed awkwardly when you hit her.'

'What?' Steph replied in disbelief. 'Oh, no. No way. I didn't do this.'

'How else do you explain this?' I asked, looking directly into her frightened eyes.

She shifted about uncomfortably on the spot. She looked unsure as whether to stay or to leave the room. When I stood up to comfort her, she backed away like I was of threat to her.

'What, you think I killed her? Can't you see I've been trying to save her? How could you think that?'

'You could've suffocated her when I went to the kitchen.'

'I said I wanted a divorce, not that I wanted her dead,' I replied, turning my back to her.

I was just about to attend to my wife once more when Steph said, 'What's that?'

'What's what?' I asked, glancing back towards her.

'It looks like there's something in her pocket,' Steph replied.

I put my hand in Alison's jean pocket and pulled out an empty bottle of prescription pills. I cursed having neither seen the bulge in her pocket nor the signs of her apparent overdose. I immediately made another desperate attempt to revive her.

Suddenly, there was a heavy knock at the front door. Steph left the room to answer it and a few seconds later the paramedics entered. I stepped away from Alison's side and the emergency medical unit went straight to work.

I don't know what I was expecting, a miracle perhaps? However, the team of professionals were unable to save my wife. Something else also ended that day: my affair with Steph. Too much had happened and too much had been said for things to go back to how they were. Both Steph and I were cleared of Alison's murder. It was declared a suicide after the post-mortem. She had taken an overdose of amphetamines before arriving home. Guilt consumes me to this day. I may not have been responsible for her murder, but it was me who killed her.

Society's Outcast

'Excuse me, sorry for interrupting, but have any of you seen this girl? She's my sister and she's been missing for almost two years now.'

The girl in the photo looked strikingly familiar. A shiver ran over me and I was lost for words.

'Her name is, Alice, Alice Brookes,' the guy said, handing me the photo.

I held the picture for a fraction too long and felt his attention bore in on me.

'I'm pretty sure this is the same girl I saw yesterday,' I said, returning the photo.

'You saw her yesterday?'

'Yeah, except she told me her name was Jenny.'

'Where did you see her?'

'Over there,' I said. Too late to get out of it now, I led him across the road.

'Thanks. My name's, Lee, Lee Brookes,' the guy said, as we walked towards the rubbish bins.

'Danny, Danny Langley,' I replied.

'What was she doing here, Danny?'

'Scrounging from a bin, I think. I've seen her in town before, but I've never taken much notice. It's only because of what happened that she caught my attention.'

'What happened?'

I recounted the story.

'Give it back!' a girl yelled. 'Give it back!'

I turned around to see three lads tossing a book they had taken from a beggar girl's pram. She had been rooting through a bin at the time of the theft, but now she was hysterical. In spite of wanting to regain her book, she stayed close to the pram, guarding it from her persecutors. They played on her disadvantage and bounced around her.

Then one of the boys managed to pull what appeared to be a baby out from the pram. However, I could see by the way he was holding it that the baby was a doll. Although it was only a toy, the girl freaked. The pram overturned with all of its contents spilling out onto the grass. The lads ran off, throwing their trophies behind them as they left.

I picked up the book and walked over to the distressed girl. She sat on the grass cradling the doll, rocking back and forth as though it were real. Kneeling down, I attempted to comfort her.

'Go away,' she said, with tears streaming from her eyes.

'I got your book,' I replied, offering it to her.

'Just put it over there,' she said, directing me with a nod.

I placed the book on the ground beside her and started to walk away. I glanced back, but she didn't bother to acknowledge me leaving. Although she hadn't said so much as thank you, I righted her pram and put her stuff back inside.

'Thank you,' a voice said from behind me. I turned around and saw the homeless girl smiling.

'No problem.'

She then placed the doll into the pram and asked, 'Would you mind looking after Darla for me?'

'Uh…yeah, sure.'

She started walking over to the bin.

'No! No! I'll buy you something to eat! It's on me, seriously.'

'Okay,' she muttered, and I thought there was a hint of relief in her eyes.

'There's a shop that sells sandwiches at the other end of the park. We could get some and bring them back here, if you like? I'm Danny,' I said, as we walked down the path together.

'Jenny,' she replied, now with a smile.

We sat under a tree and ate our sandwiches by the canal. There were fewer people in the park than an hour ago and the sun was beginning to fade. Neither of us had seemed to give the time of day much thought. I didn't want it to end and I was sure the same could be said for Jenny.

After checking on Darla, Jenny retrieved her book from the pram and began to write in it. Occasionally, she would peer at me with a cheeky smile and close the book whenever I tried to see what she was writing.

'Go on, what have you written?'

'Having sandwich in the park with Danny. See?' she said, flashing the page to me.

'So, I'm cute, am I?'

'I didn't think you'd see that.'

'Anything else in there that I might like to see?'

'I do a bit of poetry.'

'Poetry? Let's see,' I said, taking the book. Leafing through it I read:

> *Why did you abandon me?*
> *I thought that blood was thicker than water.*
> *This isn't the way it was supposed to be,*
> *After all, I'm your only daughter.*

'Rather dark, don't you think?'

'Not all of my poems are dark. Listen to this,' Jenny said, taking the book back.

> *'As free as the wind you soar through the sky,*
> *The summer is gone, now it's time to say goodbye,*
> *You'll miss the winter and all of the snow,*
> *The weather will be better when you get back, I know.*

'I wrote that on a particularly nice day, but even that day hasn't been as good as today.'

And then she leaned over and kissed me. There was real warmth in her kiss and it was a sentiment that was shared. We were having a great time and I felt like we were connecting. How could someone so wonderful end up on the streets?

'Jenny, can I ask you something?'

'Sure.'

'What happened? Why did you leave home?'

Her face dropped.

'I got pregnant. I was fifteen at the time. Needless to say, Mum and Dad were less than pleased, so they kicked me out. My boyfriend had already dumped me and he refused to accept that the baby was his, so I was on my own.'

'What happened to the baby?'

'I guess, some things aren't meant to be. You know, even though I was on my own, I was still looking forward to being a mother. I could care for her and be with her all the time. We would've been best friends and I'd never have turned her away from me, no matter what she may have done. When you lose that special someone, you feel empty inside. I would've called her Darla.'

I put my arm around Jenny and tried to comfort her. I got the impression that she hadn't been able to release her emotions before that moment. I think she appreciated my being there even after the tears had stopped.

I changed the subject and we talked about other things. She asked me about my family and she told me of the places she had been. We laughed, we joked, and before we knew it the sun had set. I had to get back but I didn't want to leave.

'I've got to go,' I said, looking to the sky.

'I know,' Jenny said, 'tonight I go to Rossitto's. The owner lets me have some of the leftovers and he even gives me a drop of wine.'

I felt torn, torn between what I had to do and what I wanted to do. If I stayed much longer, my parents would start to worry. I felt sick and there was no cure to my ailment.

'You could come with me. You could stay at mine.'

'In a three-bedroom house, with one bedroom occupied by your two sisters and another by your parents? I'm sure they'd be thrilled to have me sleep on their couch.'

'I could sneak you in. You could stay in my room. I'd be happy to sleep on the floor.'

'Sorry, Danny. Trust me, I'd really like to sleep in a nice warm bed, but if I'm going to meet your family, I'd like to meet them in better circumstances.'

She was right and I had known it all along. Reluctantly, I accepted that we would have to part company for the night.

Helping Jenny to her feet, I said, 'Can I see you again? Perhaps we could do the same tomorrow?'

'I'd like that, but tomorrow is Saturday. I make most of my money on a Saturday, so I'll be in town all day. I could see you here after five for an hour or two?'

'Great, I could take you somewhere to eat, maybe even somewhere like Rossitto's.'

'Thanks that would be great. I'll be able to keep that thought with me all day. It'll be something to look forward to. Thank you, Danny.'

We were still holding hands and, before saying goodbye, she kissed me again. The second was as nice as the first, but this time the warmth of our feelings would last until we next met. As we parted hands, we parted company, but we had only gone a few feet before I made one last plea.

'Jenny, I want you to have some of this,' I said, taking my wallet out of my pocket.

'Keep it,' she replied. 'You'll need it for tomorrow.'

'And that's the last I saw of her,' I said to Lee.

I could tell by the way he was shifting about that he didn't want to wait until five to see his sister. However, I could also tell that Lee wanted my help with finding her and was thinking of the best way to ask.

'In town, didn't you say? You wouldn't mind helping me to find her, would you, Danny?'

I had reservations about going into town, but once there I was teeming with anxiety. I was eager to see Jenny, but I was also afraid that my visit would be an intrusion and wondered, would she be pleased to see me? More important, did she want to see Lee?

Then I saw her. She was standing in an alley between two shops, with her pram to the side of her and a hat full of change in front of her. She was reciting poetry from her book.

Then she saw me and my fears were put at ease. She held a beaming smile and closed her book. She put her hand to her face, gesturing for us to get a bite to eat. Then she saw her brother. She was no longer smiling.

She picked up her hat, collected Darla from her pram and ran off down the alley. Lee gave chase with me following behind, but Jenny was a good twenty yards ahead of us. She ducked into another alley and that's where we lost her.

I crashed into some guy as I entered the tunnel and found myself on the ground at his feet. I dusted myself off and apologised to the stranger, but I was out of the running. There was no chance for me to catch up now.

Lee continued to chase after his sister, but I could tell that he was having no luck. I heard him shout 'Alice' several times in the distance. That was the last I saw of Lee and of Jenny.

I walked back to where Jenny had left her pram. I stayed there until 4:30pm, but she didn't return for it. I took the pram to the park and waited under our tree, where we said we would meet, but five o'clock came and went. To top it all off, I lost my wallet. It must have fallen out of my pocket when I had bumped into the man in the tunnel. At least I still had my phone.

I rang my mum and told her that I would be late home so I could look for my wallet. In truth, I didn't bother going back for it. Instead, I went to Rossitto's to see if she'd been there. As I expected, the owner of the restaurant told me she hadn't. I walked around aimlessly, talking to other vagrants. Eventually, I had to admit defeat and headed home. When I got there, I went straight to my bedroom. Then I cried.

Three days later I received a package in the mail. I opened it and to my surprise inside was my wallet. The money was gone, but in its place was a note:

> *Hi Danny, I've moved on. I hope you don't mind, but I have taken the thirty pounds. You did offer and I could use it. I want you to know that I don't think any less of you for bringing my brother to me. You won't understand, but he's one of them and I can't let them find me. I have your address, so I will send you another letter soon. I'm going to go to one of those cafes and set*

up an e-mail address so we can keep in touch and if you want to come up and meet me, perhaps we could have that evening out. I was looking forward to it. Sorry for standing you up.

Your friend
Jenny
xxx

Speed Dating

'Hi, I'm Angie.'

'Tom.'

'I like to fuck,' she said.

'I beg your pardon?'

'I like to fuck and you look desperate. How long has it been?'

'Close to four years, if you must know.'

'Sounds to me like you could use a good time. Why don't we put an end to this charade and spend the rest of the hour somewhere a little more cosy?'

'Uh, thanks for the offer, but I'm looking for a little bit more to a relationship then just sex. I'm new to this and I feel rather nervous and, quite frankly, you scare me. Good luck with the next date. I hope you find someone more adventurous.' Just then the buzzer sounded to move to the next table.

'Hi, I'm Brenda.'

'Tom.'

'Divorced?'

'Widowed, my wife died two years ago.'

'How long were you married?'

'Twelve years.'

'My, that was a long time. Was it your first marriage?'

'Yes.'

'None of my marriages lasted for more than a couple of years. The last one ended after ten months. I've been married four times. They always seem to start well, then I discover what they're really like and none of them took my advice. Take a look at yourself, for instance. You could use a haircut and your tie doesn't match your shirt. In fact, I don't like anything you're wearing.'

'I like this tie. My wife gave it to me. It reminds me of her and she never had a problem with how I dress.'

'Well, take it from me, it's unflattering. Now if we were together, I wouldn't let you leave the house unless you wore clothes that complement me. Don't get me wrong, I don't think a man should be subservient, but a man should be kept on a tight lead. Leave them without guidance and they stray off the path. I went through two marriages before I learnt my lesson from that one.'

'Go figure. Oh, was that the buzzer? Doesn't time fly? Nice to have met you,' I said as I got up from the table.

Sat at the next table was a young lady with a serious look on her face. Her arms were crossed and she was looking down at her watch. I slid into my seat and introduced myself.

'Hi, I'm Tom.'

'No, you won't do. I can tell by your eyes, something's not right.'

'My eyes, what's wrong with my eyes?'

'They're too blue and leering. You're either a pervert or a cop. Are you a police officer?'

'No, I'm not.'

'I should've known. Say no more. I'm like a magnet for the nutcase. So what's your fetish, breasts, legs or a nice ass? No, don't tell me. I'd rather not know.'

I made an attempt to settle her fears, but she was having none of it.

'Save it, I'm leaving. I should have known this was a bad idea. Good day, weirdo,' she said getting out of her seat. She stood up and sidled away, avoiding turning her back to me. Very strange. Perhaps she's right? Maybe this was a bad idea.

'Hi, I'm Tom.'

'Just give me a minute. I've got to finish this text.' She put her phone down on the table a few seconds later and introduced herself, 'Hi, I'm...' Suddenly, her phone was jumping about with excitement.

'Oh hi, Jill. Yes, it's great, really going well. I'm so glad you put me up to this. Thanks. I can't wait to see you to tell you all about it. None of them have been anything alike. One was a funeral director, another was a mechanic. One was unemployed. I won't be leaving my details for him. Well, I'd better go. I've got another one sat in front of me. Yeah, speak to you later. Thanks, Jill.

'Sorry about that. My name's Kelly. I'm an office clerk. What did you say your name was?'

'Tom.'

'Hi, Tom. So what do you do for a living?'

'I'm unemployed.'

'Oh...'

We sat in silence for all of five seconds when the buzzer signalled to move tables.

'Hi, I'm Helen.'

'Tom.'

'Nice to meet you. Have you ever been speed dating before?'

'No and to be honest, I'm not impressed.'

'Neither am I. Everyone I've met is either interested in sex, been through a messy divorce or too engrossed in themselves. I only decided to try this because the idea of a blind date scares me and I'm not ready to go out with somebody I know.'

'Yeah, exactly.'

'I lost my husband three years ago and only now do I feel like I'm ready to see someone.'

'I lost my wife two years ago. If you don't mind me asking, how did your husband die?'

'In a car accident. He was coming home from work when he was hit by a lorry driver who had fallen asleep at the wheel.'

'Oh, I'm sorry.'

'These things happen, but no one ever thinks it will happen to them. I guess that's what grieving is all about, realising that everything comes to an end and understanding that there are things to look forward to in spite of being left behind.'

'Wow, I never thought of it that way.'

'How did your wife die, if you don't mind *me* asking?'

'Cancer. She fought for over a year before letting go. It was horrible to watch someone so full of life deteriorate down to nothing. Before she died she thanked me for everything I gave her and said that her only regret was that she wouldn't be able to see our two daughters grow up to be the fine young women they'll become. She made one request, she asked me to find happiness, to move on. So here I am. I don't know if I'm ready for a full-blown relationship, but I do know that I need someone who I can talk to.'

Before either of us knew it, our five minutes had elapsed. Standing at my side, waiting for me to leave the table, was Helen's next date. He was fashionable, in good shape and a few years younger than me. I got up, thanked Helen for the chat and walked away from the table.

I felt deflated. I had enjoyed every second of the five minutes I had spent with Helen, but like that moment when you invite the girl of your dreams to the floor of a high school dance, the song ends and waiting in the wings is someone else ready to cut in.

With a smile, the only woman sat on her own invited me to take a seat across from her. Her expression changed within an instant of my turning and heading straight for the exit. I'd had my fill of the speeding dating experience.

'Tom, wait!' a voice called out behind me. It was Helen. 'Leaving already? I was hoping we could meet up afterwards and arrange a date to continue our chat.'

'Are you planning to stay? There's a coffee shop across the road. I would love it if you would join me.'

'I'd love to,' she replied.

I offered her my arm and together we walked towards the exit. I overheard the conversation of the final table in passing.

'I like to fuck, and you look desperate. How long has it been?'

I couldn't help but smile.

Storm Moon

'Jack Taylor? Is that you?' the stranger asked. 'It is you. It's Tom, Tom Morris. We worked together for a couple of years. What are you doing here?'

'I live around here,' I answered, feeling uneasy.

'Out here, in the middle of nowhere? Well, I suppose somebody does. It's good to see you. Must be fifteen years or more since we last met.'

'Yes, must be about that.' I said, handing the cashier thirty dollars for the gas. 'What brings you here?'

'The fishing. Me and three of my friends have rented a cottage by the lake for the week. We've heard you can hook some great trout and pike there.'

'Actually, Tom, if you're looking to catch pike there's a lake fifty or so miles east of here. Last summer's drought wasn't too kind to us, so you would probably find better fishing there.'

'No matter, truth be known, I'm not that great a fisherman anyway. I'm just looking forward to getting on that boat and drinking a few beers,' Tom said, placing a six pack on the counter.

'Well, there's quite a few bears in these parts, nowhere near as many in Thunder Bay,' I replied.

'What's the matter, Jack? Sounds to me like you're trying to put me off.'

'Yeah, Jack, what's the matter? You know there hasn't been a reported bear attack in at least ten years,' the cashier replied, glaring at me.

'Yeah, well, just trying to look out for you, Tom. Trying to return the favour, what with you saving my life and all.'

'It was nothing. You would have done the same for me.'

'I'm trying to... Just being paranoid, I guess,' I said, catching the cashier's stare once more. Taking the hint, I turned to leave the shop. 'It was nice to see you again, Tom. Good luck with the fishing.'

Walking over to my truck, I heard Tom call out, 'Jack, hold up a second. Why don't you join me and the boys tomorrow? There's plenty of room on the boat and Geoff and the others won't mind. It would be great to catch up. We can have a laugh and pull a few bass out while we're at it.'

'Sounds great, Tom, but I really think you should do your fishing somewhere else. If I were you, I'd get your stuff together and drive to the Bay. It's not safe here. Any other time of the year and it wouldn't matter. Trust me; it's in your best interest to leave. You and your friends are not welcome,' I said, stepping into my four-by-four.

'Thanks for the advice,' Tom replied, before walking over to his car looking downcast.

As Tom got into his station-wagon, I drove alongside him and rolled down the window. 'Seriously, Tom, you'd best be on your way. It's a full moon tonight and the locals don't take kindly to strangers.'

'A full moon, eh? Now, I'm scared,' Tom said, turning on the ignition. 'I should lock all the shutters and the doors too, right?'

'That won't be enough,' I said, as he drove off.

Sitting in front of the fire, an hour later, I looked up at the clock on the mantelpiece. It was ten thirty, an hour and a half until the twenty-ninth day. The doors of my cabin were securely locked and bolted, the windows were both barred and boarded, and the furniture had been pushed up to block all exits. I was ready to wait the night out as I had done so many times before. However, this time I felt on edge. I was prepared for what was to come, but I knew the same could not be said for Tom or his friends.

I stood up and began to pace about the room. I looked at the clock once more. It was ten to eleven. What was I to do? It wasn't like I didn't try to warn him. It wasn't my fault.

I jumped with fright as the clock chimed to mark the eleventh hour. Soon the night air would be filled with the howls of the afflicted and the screams of their prey.

Moving the sofa from the door, I slid the bolts back to exit my cabin. There was still time. If Tom hadn't pressed the emergency stop on that machine sixteen years ago, I wouldn't be here now. I couldn't just leave him to the mercy of the inhuman community. I had to do something.

I jumped into my truck and raced down the lane towards the road that would take me to Tom's cottage on the lake. It was an uneven dirt track that wound through the woods. The urgency of my quest to reach my friend knotted my stomach with pain. It was a twenty-minute drive, but I was sure I could make it.

I pulled over to the side of the road and got out of the vehicle. I could see the holiday home through the trees, despite the dark. Overhead the moon shone bright, drawing barks and howls from the unearthly convergence in the forest.

Following the yowls, came the screams. I was too late. I dropped to my knees, succumbing to my anguish. Suddenly, I saw a figure running towards me. It was Tom, and he practically fell over me as he raced to get away from the evil throng invading his cabin.

'Jack, are you alright? Where's your car? We've got to get out of here!'

'Sorry, Tom.' I turned and he saw my wolf ears and deep red eyes. 'You had your chance.'

Suck On This

Rosie McCarthy. Where the hell are you now?

'Would you like any bags, ma'am?' I asked the lady at the counter. She said yes and I scanned her items.

'Rosie to the till. Rosie to the till,' I called into the Tannoy, before seeing to the next customer. I turned to Sandra on the opposite checkout and asked, 'Where's, Rosie? You called her already, didn't you?'

'Yes, sir,' she replied, 'I think she might be in the storeroom with Bridget.'

'Thanks, Sandra,' I said and attended to the next person in the line.

I had sent Rosie to help Bridget over an hour ago. Surely it couldn't have taken them that long to clean up? If she's messing around again, I'll sack her ass I swear.

As soon as the line of customers had cleared, I turned to Sandra and said, 'I'm going to the storeroom. Call if you need assistance.'

I left the counter and marched down the aisle towards the storeroom. I could feel my heart pounding almost as fast as my strides as I stomped to the back of the shop. I was heating up and had I not had to look suitably professional, I would have undone my tie to let the steam escape from my collar.

I stopped just short of the storeroom's double doors. I could so easily have announced my arrival by barging through the doors, but I wanted to catch her in the act, so I crept inside instead. I could hear laughing and I bit my lip to stop myself from venting my anger. I stood behind some racking and listened intently, waiting for the right moment to pounce.

'This sucks,' I heard Rosie say, while hearing the bristles of her broom scrape the concrete.

'Yeah it does, but we better clean this up before Wing-Ears sees it,' Bridget replied, causing Rosie to giggle.

Suddenly, Rosie stopped laughing. 'It's just work, work, work.'

'I know our lives are filled with work.'

'Fuck our lives. At least I'm off this weekend.'

'What, you're not working this weekend? How'd you manage that?'

'I told Wrinkle-Dick Wing-Ears that it's my nan's 80th on Saturday and that she lives up north.'

'Is it?'

'No, and Nan lives on the other side of town. Do you think I'm going to waste my weekend in this shithole? No way. Not me.'

'Mr Nicholls will sack you if he finds out.'

'Yeah well, one day I'll tell him to stick this broom right up his ass.'

'Yeah, right.'

'I'm telling ya, I'd stick this so far up his ass that you'd think the bristles were a moustache.'

Rosie and Bridget began to laugh uncontrollably. I was fuming. I was in a good mind to sack the pair of them, but I was understaffed and I'd at least need Bridget for the weekend. I was just about to walk out on them when I heard Bridget ask Rosie, 'So, why don't you just quit?'

"Cause I don't have anything else and, until I do, I could really do with the money. I got to pay my student loan somehow. I should work this weekend really, but fuck it, as long as I have a job to come back to, I'll be able to cover the payments.'

'Ok, here's a question for you. If Wing-Ears said to you he was letting you go, would you beg him not to?'

I remained rigid and silent.

'OMG! You would, wouldn't you?'

'No.'

'Yes you would. Admit it.'

'OK, OK, I'd ask him not to fire me and probably offer to work the next three weekends or something.'

'What if he said that he was still going to fire you? Would you ask to suck his dick?'

'Eww, like gross! I'd sooner lick the sides of the toilet then put his scabby, wrinkled, two-inch pecker in my mouth. Not even if I had a cold sore that I could add to his bell end.'

The two of them howled with laughter. They couldn't stop laughing, that is until I stepped out from behind the racking. Both of them stood as if frozen, with jaws dropped. Bridget accidently let go of her broom.

'Sorry, Mr Nicholls,' she said. 'We were just cleaning up these broken jars of coffee. I stacked all the tins like you said already.'

'Bridget, go and help Sandra out on the till. I need to have a word with Rosie.'

I waited for Bridget to leave the storeroom before I turned my attention to Rosie. I could see the dread on her face. She hunched into herself and each time her gaze met mine she would look down at the floor or to the racking beside her. I said nothing and walked towards her. She shied away from me until she no longer had anywhere to step back to. Caught between the wall and the stockpile on the shelving, Rosie dipped her head on my approach.

I stopped just short of standing on her toes. The end of my nose was close enough to the side of her shamed face that I could smell the fragrance of the body lotion she had used the night before. I leant casually against the wall above her as she huddled her arms together and silently begged for mercy.

'What's the matter, Rosie? Scared you might lose your job?' I said, trying to hide the pleasure of the moment from my tone. 'Not so big now, are we? Well, you'll have plenty of time to think on what to tell your folks during the long drive up to your nan's. Oh, that's right, she only lives on the other side of town and it's not her birthday either.'

'Look, Mr Nichols—' she tried to say before I interrupted her.

'What, not Wing-Ears?' She dropped her head, said nothing and closed tighter into the corner. I leaned over her with one hand on the wall and the other on the racking. 'Give me one reason why I shouldn't sack your sorry ass. Working the next three weekends isn't quite going to cut it. Now, you could tell me to stick my job where you suggested you'd shove your broom or you could show me just how desperate you are to maintain the payments on that student loan of yours.'

I took my hands from the wall and the shelving and slowly began to unzip my fly. She gasped in horror and stared at me in disbelief with frightened eyes. I smiled and said, 'Should we put it to the test? Would you rather suck my wrinkled two-inch pecker or lick the sides of the toilet? I'd quite like to see you do both.'

'Suck on this asshole!' I heard someone yell from behind me. I turned around and met with the coarse bristles of Bridget's broom, full in the face. I fell to the floor and banged my head on a wooden crate under the shelving.

Sitting in my office, looking at application forms, I rubbed the cuts and scratches under my nose before resting my hand on the bandage covering the stitches in my forehead. Suddenly, the phone rang. I picked up the receiver and answered all of my caller's queries.

'Yes, Rosie was a very good worker. I've had no complaints. I'm actually sorry to be losing her and I'm sure she would make an invaluable employee, like she has been for me.'

Taken In

'Help me! Please, help me! Oh God, let me in!' I yelled pulling at the locked door. I looked behind me. There was no one there, but he couldn't be far. I banged on the door again. 'Help! Open the door! Please, hurry!'

In what seemed like forever, an old man eventually answered the door. There was a look of shock on his face when I fell into the hallway.

'Shut the door! Shut the door!' I shouted, picking myself up to my knees.

'Henry! What's going on?' a woman called out from an adjoining room. Rushing to my side, the old woman comforted me as her husband closed their front door, 'Oh, you poor thing.'

'Call the police. There's a man out there trying to kill me.'

'Henry, get to the phone,' the woman said, helping me to my feet. 'Come, let's get you inside.'

I sat down on the couple's couch with the old woman at my side. She rubbed my shoulders. I was shaking.

'You're safe now. He can't get you anymore. Henry's on the phone with the police. Everything will be fine.'

'Thank you. Thank you,' I replied.

'They're on their way,' Henry said, standing in the doorway.

'Is there anything we can get you? A glass of water? Some biscuits?' the old woman asked.

'Water, water would be great.'

'Henry, could you get this young lady some water?' my host said. She continued to rub my arms while we waited for her husband to return. As he handed me my drink, she introduced herself. 'My name is Alison and this is my husband, Henry. What is your name?'

'Heather,' I answered.

'Henry and I have lived here all our lives. To think that there's a killer loose in our village... I hope the police arrive soon. What does this man look like?'

'He's tall, at least six foot in height. He's got to be about ten years older than me, say early forties. He has sandy, mop-like hair and has a deep scar down the right side of his face.'

'Good God, that sounds like Steven Rayner,' Alison said, looking dismayed. 'He only lives a few doors from here.'

'Forgive me, Heather,' Henry asked, taking a seat across from me, 'I've never seen you here before, but what are you doing in our village?'

I handed my glass to his wife and exhaled deeply. I still felt shaky, but I wanted to find out more about Steven Rayner.

'I work for the Herald. I'm a journalist. A colleague and good friend of mine was writing a piece on the disappearance of several young girls in the city.'

'But, that's eighty miles away and Henry and I watch the news and they said that the missing girls were local to Manchester.'

'Yes, Alison, but she was attacked, and who knows what Steven gets up to. He does seem rather strange.'

'I wouldn't say that he was strange, just quiet and unsociable.'

'Alison, the boy's strange. In the twenty years that he's lived at number twelve, he's not once been in the pub or shown his face at the village fete. No one ever sees him, except when he's at the shop or the petrol station. He's not right and to tell the truth, none of this comes as a surprise to me at all. Anyhow, sorry, Heather, you were saying about your friend at the Herald?'

I continued with my story. 'My friend was following a lead and came up here. He never returned.'

'You think, Steven... oh my God. I'm going to call the police again. They're taking too long,' Alison said and walked out of the room.

'Alison, they'll be here soon. Give them a chance.'

'This is an emergency, Henry,' Alison snapped.

Suddenly, there was a knock at the door.

'Oh, thank God. They're here,' I could hear Alison say from down the hall.

Henry got up and stopped his wife from answering the door. 'It might not be them.'

He walked to the door and Alison stayed put in the hall. I waited to find out who my hosts' caller was and noticed a magazine on the table. It was addressed to Alison Rayner.

I shot out of my seat. I looked to the hallway. Henry was standing at the entrance. 'The police have arrived,' he said, stepping aside.

A tall and broad officer walked into the room. He had sandy, mop-like hair and a deep scar down the right side of his face.

'Good evening, so nice of you to call in on my aunt and uncle. It's a small community, Heather. It's a very small community,' Steven said, as he walked towards me.

The Girl in the Lake

'Bleeding dog,' I cursed to myself; it wasn't like Ben to wander off. It was getting late and the weather looked as if it was about to turn, and I was still a good fifteen minutes from the Horse and Plough Inn. The last thing I needed was to spend an extra hour in the woods searching for a bedraggled spaniel and getting soaked in the process.

'Ben! Ben!' I called out before spotting him a few seconds later. 'There you are. What do you see, boy?'

He stood at the edge of the lake looking out at the water in a manner I had never seen before. As I walked over to him, he hunched, put his tail between his legs and backed away from the water's edge.

'Ben?' I walked over and knelt down beside him. As I stroked his head and patted his side, I looked out at the open expanse before me. It was clear and motionless. I saw nothing to suggest what might have spooked my sensitive springer.

Brushing the incident aside, I clipped the lead back onto Ben's collar and stood up. Suddenly, I caught a glimpse of something in the water from the corner of my eye. Leaning over to have a better look, I could see the glint of something resting on the bed of the shallows. It was just out of arm's reach, so I picked up a nearby stick and fished about in the water.

After several minutes of fumbling, I dragged out a lady's wrist watch. Though the water had got behind the glass, the gold metallic surround had dulled but not rusted, and the white strap had not deteriorated. It was a dress watch, worn for special occasions, but there were no churches or fancy restaurants around here and the path by the lake was hardly the place for a well-dressed woman to walk along.

I put the watch in my pocket and prepared to leave. Just as I was about to turn away from the lake, I noticed a sudden change in the clarity of the water. Instead of becoming murky, as one would expect from disturbing the sand on the bottom, it appeared to create a milky swirl that was slowly pulling itself together and assuming a form of some kind. Stepping up to have a better look, I gazed at the apparition taking shape in the water. There before me was the ghostly appearance of a young girl, floating about beneath the surface.

Frozen in disbelief, I stared at the translucent image. She had a youthful complexion and a kindly gaze, but with a saddened expression. The nightgown she was wearing and her dark, silky hair were drifting softly with the current. It had a hypnotic effect. She could be no older than sixteen and her pale arms swayed elegantly about the water before reaching out to me. Soundlessly calling to me with her arms stretched above her head, she slowly began to rise from the depths.

A hand emerged from the water and the sight chilled me to the bone. The hand bore no resemblance to the beauty of the girl still shrouded below the waterline. It was draped in rotting flesh. The forefinger was missing, and the others were entwined with reeds and soil that had once sat on the bottom of the mere.

Horrified, I took a step backwards only to fall onto the muddy bank. Thrashing my legs about the shallows in desperation to get up, I crawled from the waterline, re-joining my faithful companion. Sitting back on the trodden grass verge, I looked out at the lake. It was clear, still and silent. She was gone.

I stood up and persuaded Ben to recommence our walk. I upped our pace to get away from the reservoir, slowing down once the path reentered the woods.

Though I was clear of the pool, I couldn't get the image of the phantom out of my mind. The way she drifted in the water, the way our eyes engaged. The intensity of the moment left me feeling out of place. Even when the pub was in sight, I couldn't shake my unsettled mood.

I sat in my local with a pint in front of me and my dog at my side and took the watch out of my pocket. The time was fixed on 9:25pm and on the back there was an inscription, which read, 'For our loving daughter, Elizabeth.' There were also the remnants of a stain by the clasp, possibly a result of submersion.

Inside the pub there were two old boys who were there every night, and as usual they were sat at the bar watching the news on the TV.

'And in other news tonight, police are still looking for the missing school girl, Elizabeth Wolsey, who went missing from her high school prom three days ago. Police are asking anyone with information on her whereabouts to please come forward.'

I immediately thought about the girl in the lake. It had to be her. She had been too real for me to have made her up, to have imagined her. The watch must have been hers and she had led me to it. The news report said she was missing, but I now knew different. I just didn't expect to be the one to locate the body.

I went out into the car park before ringing the police. Half an hour later and I was guiding the authorities to where I had found the watch. They asked me a number of questions, but I never mentioned the spectre I had seen in the water. I must have seemed shaken to them, but I'm sure they must have thought it was a result of finding the evidence of a dead girl.

The following night I was forced to take a different route to the pub. I kept Ben on the lead and the police had cornered off the section of the lake where I had found the watch. Despite having to take an alternate path, the memory of my ghostly encounter was still fresh in my mind.

The path ran alongside the mere at various points, but I kept my eyes focused on the way ahead. Nevertheless, at the point where I passed closest to the lake, I could not help but take a quick glance across the open water. To my horror, I noted something vertical sticking out from its calm surface. I couldn't make out what it was, but I was sure that it was something unnatural. I turned my head away and looked to the trees ahead of me.

I stopped in my tracks. I didn't want to, but something compelled me to have another look. Gazing across the reservoir, my jaw dropped. There, fifty yards or so out in the open, was a girl dressed in a filthy night gown, standing on top of the water. Fortunately, she was far enough away that I knew she could do me no harm.

Her matted hair was draped over her face and was adorned with plants from the lakebed and she stood motionless with her arms at her side. I didn't need to see her close up; her image was clear in my mind. I shuddered before taking control of my senses and racing into the woods ahead of my dog. I didn't look back; I knew she was still there, but why was she haunting me?

Back in the pub and the old boys were there like they had never left. I sat at the same table, with my pint at the ready, but I didn't feel much like drinking it. To me it was like I had just attended someone's funeral, and I never drank at wakes.

'I hear they got the guy who killed that girl,' one of the old boys said to the other pointing up to the TV. 'Fancy dumping her in our lake. I'm surprised anyone from the city knows it's there.'

'That's 'cause her killer was Chris Holloway.'

'Chris who?'

'Chris Holloway. He used to live at Stork Cottage. He came up from the city, lived there for a couple of years and then went back down. Lived there about ten years ago.'

'I know him. Didn't he have a daughter that lost a finger?'

'That's him and rumour has it that she went missing a few years later. You know, it wouldn't surprise me if they find a few more bodies in that lake.'

The old boy was right. The police found the bodies of three more missing girls, including Mr Holloway's daughter. Since then, I haven't seen her apparition by the lake, instead she visits my dreams, but in my dreams she is smiling.

The Money

'Where's the money?!' Lou yelled at Bobby who was tied to a wooden chair. Lou had worked Bobby over real good, but in spite of the pounding Bobby remained tight lipped.

'Where's the fucking money?!' Lou yelled, before nailing Bobby with a hard right hook. Lou hit him so hard that if he hadn't been wearing knuckledusters I'm sure he would have broken his hand.

Bobby spat a wad of blood on the stone floor, looked up and in a slurred voice replied, 'Fuck you, man! Fuck you!'

Lou was angry. He didn't say anything, but I could tell he was mad. We had taken a few of Mr Ferlizzo's clients into the basement before and all had talked. This was getting us nowhere but Lou was not about to be defeated.

'Chris, take down his trousers,' Lou said to me, turning his back on the blood-soaked 'job' sitting beneath the single light bulb illuminating the room. 'Take down his trousers. I'm going to get a spoon.'

'A what?' I asked, as my six-foot-four-inch-tall, partner ascended the stairs.

'Don't worry about it. Just get him ready. I'll be back in a few minutes.'

Lou left me alone with Mr Ferlizzo's bloodied client. Bobby looked a mess. His face was completely swollen, his jaw broken, there was blood running from the right side of his mouth and his left eye was closed up. He had had enough and yet he was not talking. If it weren't for the fact that I was hardened to this sort of thing, I would have pitied the man.

'Where's the money, Bobby?' I asked, unfastening his belt.

'Fuck you, fuck you,' Bobby replied.

'Don't be stupid. I don't know what he has in mind, but unless you tell me where the money is, when Lou gets back you're going to find out what pain really is.'

Lou returned to the basement a few minutes later with a spoon, a blowtorch and a pair of pliers. He sported a self-satisfied grin and walked over to Bobby.

'Have you ever been kicked in the nuts, Bobby? I'm sure you have. Well, this is going to hurt a whole lot more,' Lou said, firing up the blowtorch. 'Where's the money?'

'It's in my apartment,' Bobby suddenly answered.

'Where?'

'Behind the mirror, in my home office, there's a safe.'

'What's the combination?'

'1066.'

'See, Chris, I knew he would cooperate. Here, hold this,' Lou said, handing me the blowtorch.

'What are you doing?'

'Well, I've heated it up now. You don't think I'm just going to let it cool down?'

I turned away. A second later I heard the most piercing scream that Bobby was now able to produce. When the noise stopped, I noticed Lou standing beside me. I glanced at Bobby. He appeared to have passed out, but was convulsing.

Bang! Bang! Bang!

Three shots rang out from Lou's revolver.

'What are you doing?!' I yelled, after the shell casings had hit the floor.

'What?' Lou replied, guiltless over what he had done.

'Mr Ferlizzo said that he wanted him brought back alive!'

'It doesn't matter. We know where the money is. Five million can go quite far in Mexico or Brazil.'

'What are you saying?'

'I'm saying, we can collect the money and make our way to South America. Are you with me or are you not?'

It didn't take me a second to answer. He had a gun and he wouldn't need much convincing to use it.

'Yeah, I'm in, but I hope you know what you are doing. If we don't report back in a couple of hours, they'll come looking for us.'

'Don't worry. We'll go to Bobby's apartment, collect the money and go straight to the airport. By the time Mr Ferlizzo gets wind of what we're doing, we'll be on a plane to wherever. When we get there, we'll buy a car and he'll have no idea of where to find us. Come on. Let's get to Bobby's.'

Lou and I headed straight for Bobby's apartment, a ten-minute drive. I was silent the whole way. Thoughts of getting the money and leaving were at the forefront of my mind. Mr Ferlizzo would be furious and what Lou had done to Bobby would be nothing compared to what would be in store for us if we were to get caught.

Bobby's place was very luxurious, but neither of us stood around to admire it. There was a large wall-hung mirror where Bobby had said it would be. Taking the mirror off the wall, Lou revealed the safe and punched in the combination.

'What the fuck?!' Lou yelled, stepping back in surprise. Though the safe was not empty, it didn't contain the cash he had expected.

I walked over and looked inside. There was a folder of paperwork, an expensive watch, a USB stick and a pair of ringside tickets for a championship fight. The consequences of coming away empty handed entered my mind, but in spite of this I kept cool. Lou wasn't so calm.

'Bobby, you fucking asshole!' Lou shouted, hurling a desktop computer across the room.

'Lou, take it easy! Calm down for fuck's sake!' I yelled at the big man.

'Calm down?! There's no money, Chris! We're fucked!'

'Look, go search his bedroom while I look through this folder. There might be something here that will tell us where the money is.'

Lou walked off as angry as ever, but my reasoning had got through to him. Though he was seething he left the room, and without throwing anything else.

I took the folder from the safe, set it on the desk and leafed through it. The paperwork was a record of business transactions between various organisations, all of which were a direct link to Carlos Ferlizzo. It was the kind of information that could put quite a few people away for a very long time.

I closed the folder and went to the safe to clear it of its contents. I could hear Lou venting his frustrations as I put the USB stick and the watch in my pockets. Suddenly, I noticed that there was a set of keys within the safe. I looked at the desk and tried one of the keys. One of the base drawers opened. Inside, there was a supply of stationery and cartridge inks. I tried another key. Bingo, account details and a cheque book for an overseas bank.

'Nothing! Fucking nothing!' Lou exclaimed, as he came back into the room.

Smiling, I said, 'Bobby's got a Swiss bank account.'

'Right, let's go,' Lou replied.

'Go where?'

'To the airport.'

'We can't just go to the airport,' I said angrily, 'I haven't got my passport for one thing.'

'Shit!' Lou replied. It was getting late and there wasn't enough time to collect our passports.

'Don't panic,' I said, in as calm a manner as I could muster, 'I can wire the money to us. We needn't leave the country. All we need is a computer. We'll have to go and buy one now that you destroyed Bobby's, but we can get one before checking into a hotel somewhere.'

Like the drive to Bobby's apartment, the journey to the hotel was silent. We were both anxious to get out of the city and neither of us would be able to relax until we did. We stopped off at an electronics superstore and picked up a laptop before hitting the motorway. Mr Ferlizzo was sure to know by now and would be hunting for us.

We drove west for an hour and a half. We needed to check into somewhere rural. Ferlizzo had eyes everywhere, especially within the towns surrounding the city. All I needed was a good internet connection to transfer the money and ensure our safety.

We got ourselves a double room that had everything we needed, including a desk where I could setup the laptop. I told Lou that it would take time to get the computer going and go through Bobby's accounts. I also had to crack his passwords and that would be no easy task. Fortunately, Lou left me to get on with the job and adjourned to the hotel bar.

Lou returned a couple of hours later. Although I had located the money, overcoming the passwords was proving to be difficult. I eventually conceded defeat at just after one in the morning, telling Lou that I would try again at the next hotel. I climbed into bed and closed my eyes. Though I was tired, I couldn't sleep. Ferlizzo's men were sure to find us; it was only a matter of time.

Crash!

The breaking of the room's door woke Lou within an instant, but before he or I could do anything, we were dragged out of bed, me by my hair. Lying face down on the carpet, I tilted my head to the left. I could see two of Ferlizzo's men restraining Lou with cable ties and duct tape.

We were thrown into the back of a van and accompanied by four of Mr Ferlizzo's heavies. Though Lou and I were silent, the journey was not a quiet one. Both Lou and I were subject to relentless taunts all the way back to the soundless environment of Mr Ferlizzo's dim cellar. No captive taken to the cellar had ever left alive and the taunts were reflective.

'So, you thought you could do me out of five million? How wrong you were,' Ferlizzo said, as he descended the stairs into the cellar. Pointing towards me he said, 'Untie him.'

Helped from my chair, I stood before the big man himself. He smiled, but said nothing, waiting for an explanation.

'Everything you need is on the USB stick. Access codes, passwords, account numbers, it's all there.'

'Thank you, Christopher. You did the right thing by sending me that e-mail. Wait for me in my study. We'll discuss the rewards of your loyalty shortly.'

Mr Ferlizzo patted me on the back before turning his attention to Lou. Lou was a dead man. Just before exiting the low-lit room, I heard Mr Ferlizzo instruct two of his heavies, 'Bruno, loosen him up. Gino, fetch me a blow torch and a spoon.'

The Myth in the Cellar

'Chicken? Boc, boc, boc,' Nick said, pushing me towards the boarded up house in front of us.

'Yeah, you chicken, Mike? He's chicken,' Ron stated, turning to the four of us standing on the drive.

The three-bedroom detached house was in a sorry state. It was weather-beaten and had several missing roof tiles. The paintwork was peeling and the lawn was overgrown and unkempt. Wooden panels covered the windows and doors, the steps leading up to the porch were cracked and the number plaque was hanging by one screw. Its exterior appearance certainly lived up to its reputation for being haunted. I wasn't scared—I was petrified, and stood speechless contemplating the task before me.

'Well, go on then. If you want to be one of us, you know what you have to do,' Chris, the leader of the group, said. All were there to goad me along, with the exception of Dean who was grounded for the weekend.

Slowly, I walked up the weed-strewn drive towards the house. Instinct was telling me to turn and run and ignore what my friends would say the next day at school, but my will propelled me forward. I didn't want to lose face and I was desperate to be accepted into the gang. In spite of my fear, I was determined to enter the infamous killer's house and complete my initiation by touching the furnace at the back of the cellar.

Moving around the dilapidated porch, I headed for the back door. Before slipping around the corner, I glanced over my shoulder at my friends and they gestured for me to get on with it. The rumours of what had gone on down in the cellar played on my mind.

If the front of the property was in a sorry state, then the back was even worse. Broken glass from the smashed window littered the border next to the only door. The door hung on rusted hinges and though an adult would struggle to squeeze through its narrow gap, for a young adolescent like me it was a cinch.

I slipped through and found myself in what had been the kitchen, only most of the fittings had been stripped out. The only source of light came from the broken window behind me. The sun's weak rays highlighted a few of the dust-covered worktops and dirty wooden floorboards. There was an open doorway that appeared to lead into an unremarkable lounge, but it was the lone door to the right that I was looking for.

Although there was paint flaking from it, the door was sturdy and intact. I opened the door, and to my horror I found the cellar beneath lay in complete darkness. I stood for a moment and contemplated whether to proceed down into its depths. Taking a deep breath, I placed my hand on the wall and took my first step.

The wooden board creaked loudly and bowed under my weight. Though I was pretty sure it would support me, the movement and noise added to my trepidation and I took care with each step, ensuring my stability before proceeding to the next. My heart was racing and my eyes were wide open, though they may as well have been shut for all I could see.

Down on the stone basement floor, I began to shake. The air was damp and still, enveloping me in an eerie silence. A shiver ran down my spine. This was the den of Peter Skinner, the infamous child killer who used to eat his victims and throw their bones to his dog. The furnace that he used to char what little remained was somewhere at the back of the cellar.

I moved into the darkness, my anxiety growing with each step. I walked with my arms outstretched, feeling the air before me.

Within a few seconds of wading in the dark, I became aware I was not alone. At first, I thought it was my imagination, but then I could hear something, almost feel it. The soft wheezing noise gradually got louder. I froze and strained my ears. It was breathing. There was someone—or something—in this room with me.

Suddenly, I was grabbed by the shoulders. I screamed in horror, 'Aghhhh!' I tried to break free, but I couldn't seem to shake its grasp. Then with a hideous laugh, I was let go and a familiar voice said, 'God, Mikey, can you ever scream. Boy, I wish I could see your face!'

'Very funny,' I replied, my heart still racing. 'I could've died of fright, Dean.'

'Oh, lighten up. It was just a bit of fun. Anyway, well done, you're in.'

'I'm in?'

'Yeah, you're in.'

In spite of the eerie nature of my surroundings and the fact that Dean's practical joke had taken several years off my life, I suddenly felt elated. I had completed my initiation. I was one of the gang! Sure, my friends would laugh at me, but they would all surround me, pat me on the back and welcome me into the fraternity.

'Come on, let's get back, just give me a second to get my torch out,' Dean said, putting a hand on my shoulder to steady himself, as he shuffled through his pockets.

Suddenly, a sound like a tin can being knocked against the floor resounded around the cellar walls. My feelings of exhilaration changed to fear again.

'Was that you, Mike?' Dean asked, the anxiety obvious in his tone.

'Quit messing around,' I yelled, in no mood to be the subject of any further pranks.

'I'm not messing about. I'm serious,' Dean replied.

Dean turned on his pocket-sized torch and slowly scanned the room in search of the source of the noise. I could see the furnace on the far wall and a few items lying on the floor, including an overturned can of pop. I hoped that our intruder was a rat or a mouse, but we could see nothing. An overwhelming desire to leave the cellar consumed me.

'Let's get out of here,' I said.

'Yeah, let's go!'

Suddenly, Dean screamed, 'Ahhhhh!' His torch dropped to the floor and skidded in the direction of the furnace before stopping at the wall, illuminating a small patch of the breezeblock surface.

'Mikey, help! Get help! Mikey! Mi—' Dean's plea was shrill and desperate, and had been cut short. This was no joke. Overcome with fear, I stood rigid in the eerie silence.

'Dean? Dean?' I called out in a whisper, but to no avail. Dean didn't respond. Where was he? What had happened to him? I couldn't see him, couldn't feel him anymore.

A profound sense of dread overwhelmed me. I knew he was gone and I wouldn't see him again. I blindly bolted for the stairs behind me. Tripping on the first step, I fell forward on the wooden flight, saving myself with my hands. Pain shot through my wrist, but I didn't care as I scrabbled up the stairway as fast as I could, my panic driving me on. Clambering to the top, I caught my right ankle between two steps. I shook my leg frantically to free it, but it wouldn't budge. To my horror I heard something coming up the stairs behind me.

All of a sudden, my leg was free. I could move! Too late! My leg was being clasped by the unknown entity in the dark below. My fingernails scraped along the board of the top step as I resisted being pulled back into the cellar. Losing hold, I screamed, 'Help! Aghhhhhhhh! Aghhhhhhhh!—'

'Keep hold of him, will you! I can't administer the tranquiliser with him thrashing around like this!' the doctor exclaimed, holding a needle aloft, away from my flailing arms.

'I'm trying!' said the nurse.

'Security! Somebody call security!' the doctor barked, prompting another nurse to call for assistance.

Soon I was pinned to the floor by two hospital security men and a porter, while the doctor administered the drugs to sedate me. I was carted off to a place where I could do no harm either to myself or others. It wasn't the first time in twenty years that I had found myself in the padded room of Showell Institution, and it wouldn't be the last.

The Portrait

What do you see?

You see a man standing proud, dressed in his finest for one of the most significant achievements of his life. He wears a black gown, accompanied by a blue hood and red stole, draped over a well-tailored suit, sporting a white carnation. A flat, wide-brimmed cap sits on his head with its tassel hanging over the left side of his face.

A face that gleams like the radiant light around him. He is both handsome and mature, reflecting the wisdom of his middle age. He is neither thickset nor lean, and though his height is indiscernible, the scale of the cathedral backdrop would suggest that he is average.

His mousey hair is short, his face well kempt and his smile welcoming. His blue eyes draw you towards his kindly heart. His posture is proud and he stands as one at home amid the grandeur of the occasion.

They say that a picture tells a thousand words, but what was Mona Lisa thinking when she sat for Da Vinci?

What do I see?

I see a man holding a false smile, straining under the weight of the anguish that has brought him to the brink of collapse. With only the praise of his peers to sustain him, he hides the shame overwhelming him. Struggling to accept that his life is of equal value to that of the managers and directors who beat his self-worth into a meaningless existence, he stands humble and full of pride in spite of the burden of his suffering.

I see a man who recognised that suicide was not an option and who believed that ends would bring new beginnings.

The Runway Saloon

Pulling into the parking lot of the Runway Saloon, the boys and I stepped out of the car for a typical Friday night at the peelers. I could feel the excitement coursing through my veins. Like the feeling you get before entering a stadium for a concert, the anticipation of the event put me on an instant high. This was much better than going to the pictures or playing pool and it was far more erotic then any cheap thrill you could get from watching a porno. This was live, unadulterated flesh and the VIP room was beckoning.

The four of us walked through the chrome-handled doors and past its two large attendants with ease. Once beyond the entrance hall, the club opened out, inviting us to take a seat.

Jack went to the bar while the rest of us went in search of a table close to the stage. We had to shimmy past another huge bouncer on our way to our chairs, but we were soon seated and facing the current act on display.

Like all the strippers, she was fit, sunbed-tanned and model-like. The stunning girl on stage was no longer wearing the matching bra that went with her G-string. She had long, dark, silky hair, supple legs and shapely breasts. She crawled teasingly on the floor towards those in the front row and winked or licked her lips to those sitting at the tables behind.

Jack had returned with the beers and took a seat between Nigel and Mark. He hollered his appreciation for the dancer on stage before sitting down. Beer in hand, we all said cheers and settled down to watch the show.

It wasn't long before our company was interrupted by one of the many strippers inviting patrons to partake in a private dance. Jack grabbed the chance and followed her to the VIP lounge. A few minutes later and our table was visited by another of the evening's entertainment. This time our guest had caught my eye.

My voluptuous host was the girl who had been on stage. Now she was wearing heels and the top half of her matching undergarments. I took little persuasion to accept her offer.

'Would you like a dance?'

Her voice was soft and alluring. She had an Eastern European accent and she made her plea with such persuasive subtly that I couldn't say no.

'Sure,' I replied.

'Here or in the lounge?' she asked with a wink, placing emphasis on a more intimate session.

'The lounge would be great,' I replied, grinning from ear to ear.

As I moved out from my chair Nigel asked my escort, 'How much does it cost for a dance?'

She leant down to him and asked him to repeat his question over the volume of the in-house music. As they spoke, I leered at her, examining every detail of her delectable figure. She was mine for as long as I wanted and I was the envy of every man in the establishment, including my friends.

'Ten pounds or fifteen in the lounge,' she said, before standing up and putting her arm in mine.

The lounge was up a short flight of stairs at the back of the club. It was dimly lit and the noise from the floor and the music were not as overpowering. The chairs were more luxurious than the plain wooden ones by the stage and there was a small table by each one for setting your beer.

I eased myself into the plush armchair. My attractive host pulled up a short stool and sat across from me. She had a warm innocence about her that was most appealing. I smiled and introduced myself.

'Tony,' I said, outstretching my hand.

'Zofia,' she replied.

'Zofia, what a lovely name.'

'You're so sweet,' she answered, touching my thigh. She stood up and started to dance as the first song commenced.

She swayed seductively to the rhythm of the music, captivating my attention and arousing me. Teasingly, she removed her bra and ran it over my shoulder, before placing it on the table beside me, next to her purse. Occasionally, she perched herself on my lap and gyrated on my groin.

She stepped out of her G-string just as the song ended. She smiled and asked, 'Would you like another dance?'

'Yes please,' I replied and Zofia got down to business.

Resting on my loins more frequently than before, she pulsated upon me. Mindful not to get me too hot under the collar, she stood up and whispered in my ear.

'We can do a lot more if you stay for five songs.'

Zofia kicked one of her legs up onto the headrest of my chair and thrust her shaven pussy into my face. Though I'm sure she had expected me to sample her essence, unlike Adam, I resisted the forbidden fruit.

How many other men had taken Zofia up on her offer? How many men had put their mouth where she was suggesting? I was completely put off. I was no kerb crawler.

When the song ended, I thanked Zofia for the dance and put thirty pounds on the table. She picked up the money and asked, 'Where's the rest?'

'Two songs, thirty quid,' I replied and stood up.

'You had three songs and it's forty-five,' she said, no longer the warm host she had been a moment ago.

'No, I had two dances and that's all you're getting,' I replied in a similarly frosty manner. I then made my way out of the lounge with Zofia yelling obscenities as she rushed to get dressed.

Before long, I was sitting back at the table with my friends. They could see that I was quiet and knew better than to speak to me. Had Jack been back from the lounge, I would have convinced them all to head out for the next bar. Instead, I sat in silence and pondered over my anger.

Zofia hadn't seen me as a person; she had seen me as money. She had played on my longings and had urged me on. She couldn't have cared less if she had taken all that my wallet had to offer. And what was she thinking while she was perched on my lap? Was she laughing while she thought about what she would buy with the money I'd paid? She made me feel sick and I tarred all of her kind with the same brush.

Glancing over my shoulder, I caught sight of Zofia at the base of the stairs to the VIP lounge. She was with a bouncer and she was pointing in my direction.

Great, here we go, but to my surprise the bouncer simply waved Zofia away. Perhaps it was because she had tried to swindle patrons before or maybe it was because haggling over one dance was neither worth the hassle nor his concern. Either way, Zofia looked less than pleased and sauntered off in search of her next customer.

I didn't have to suggest moving on to the next bar, Jack did so on his return from the lounge. We ended up in this place called JP's and shot some pool. I didn't play very well, I kept thinking about Zofia. She may not have looked at me as a human being, but I'd hardly looked at her with the same regard. To me she was little more than a cheap thrill on a night out. How could I denigrate her morals in comparison with mine? I won't lie and say that I didn't visit another strip joint, but I never went to the VIP lounge again, nor the Runway Saloon.

Those Eyes

With a bag of groceries hanging off either handle of my daughter's pushchair and another two in my right hand, I steered Hannah towards the supermarket's exit. Within a few seconds of leaving the store, she began to cry, having lost her doll. Looking back I could see it lying just outside the entrance. I cursed and pulled my loaded stroller back towards the shop.

Setting the bags in my hand aside, I turned to collect my daughter's toy. Just as I was about to lean down to get it, a kindly gentleman came to my aid.

'I got it,' he said.

Our eyes met as he stood up before me and a shiver ran over the whole of my body. His eyes were strikingly familiar and I knew that instant that they belonged to a man I hadn't seen in fifteen years. I stood frozen to the spot. My stomach turned. I was speechless.

I couldn't remember what his name was, but it was him. His hair had thinned, he had put on weight and he now wore a moustache, but it was undeniably him. I wouldn't have recognised him had it not been for his eyes. Those eyes, those unforgettable eyes.

It was like I was staring into the past. Gazing into the eyes of a stranger who once stopped me from falling to the floor at an off-campus party. I was holding a glass of wine in one hand and a shot in the other. I fell into his arms, we giggled, then we kissed. I prayed that he didn't remember me. Why, Hannah, why did you have to drop your doll?

'There you go,' he said, handing it to me. He looked me up and down. 'Don't I know you?'

'I don't think so,' I replied and dipped my head in shame. I gave the doll back to Hannah and thanked the man while I still had my back to him.

'Forgive me, but I'm sure I know you from somewhere. Do you work at the bank?'

'No, I don't work. I haven't worked in years,' I replied, picking up the shopping bags from next to the stroller.

'Sorry, I didn't mean to make you feel uncomfortable. It's just that... my son goes to cubs near here. Do you have a son that..?'

'No, I don't have any sons. Thanks again,' I said and resumed with my journey towards the car park.

I made my way to my car as quickly as I was able. He didn't ask any further questions, but even so I could feel his eyes burning into the back of my head. Thank goodness he couldn't read my thoughts or sense my anguish. If he could, he would recall the game of truth or dare we played all those years ago and spin the bottle later that same night. Please, God, don't let him remember or call out to me. Please, just let this moment pass and let me get to my car without having to speak to him again.

I didn't need to look back to know he was still behind me and, wouldn't you know it, his car was parked a few yards across from mine. He smiled, but said nothing as he walked past and I returned the compliment as best I could.

I strapped Hannah into her car seat, and then put her pushchair and the shopping in the boot. I sat behind the wheel, put the keys in the ignition and looked across the car park. He was gone.

I breathed out and rested my head on the steering wheel for a moment. Time, marriage and children had enabled me to put him and others out of my mind. I had done my best to forget about my days of uni and my drug and alcohol fuelled escapades of revelry and sex without attachment. I was so naive. I never gave it a second thought back then. How could I have been so stupid?

'Drink, Mummy, drink,' Hannah said from behind me.

I looked in the rear view mirror and she was smiling. I smiled back before digging through my handbag to find her bottle. Handing it to her, I turned the key and drove out of the car park. It was a five-minute drive to get home, but in that time the thought of him and my past consumed me.

As it had with so many other parties, the merriment had intensified. We were both sitting on the floor across from each other, dressed in our underwear. Someone spun the bottle; it pointed to me. Instead of removing my bra, I stood up, walked over to him and held out my hand. I stared into his eyes, those striking blue expressive eyes, as I helped him to his feet. Hand in hand we adjourned to the bedroom. I snuck out a few hours later and caught a taxi home, where the memory of our consensual passion faded into my pillow like so many before him.

Back home, I placed Hannah in front of the TV and went to the kitchen to put away the groceries. Stacking a tin of beans at the back of the pantry, I heard the front door open. Kelsey, my other daughter had returned from school.

'Hi, Mum,' she called out from the hall. I then heard her speaking to Hannah. I shut the pantry door and slumped into a chair at the table.

'Mum, are you okay?' Kelsey asked, on entering the kitchen. 'What's wrong?'

I looked up at my teenage daughter and I immediately sensed her concern from the sadness in her eyes. Those eyes, those striking blue expressive eyes. I wiped mine and stood up before answering her in an assured tone, 'Nothing's wrong. I'm fine. I was just feeling a little emotional. Come here and give me a hug.'

Trick or Treat

'Trick or treat!' said the goblin, the witch and the spaceman.

'My, aren't we all horrible,' I replied. 'Alright then, how about a trick?'

I glanced at the scarecrow lying on the porch behind them and sported a smug grin as my husband rose wearing the most hideous of carved pumpkins. He placed a hand on the goblin's and spaceman's shoulders.

'Ahhhh!' the kids screamed as they stumbled down our steps to get away.

'That's right! Run as fast as you can and don't ever come back!' I hollered, before sharing a laugh with my husband.

'That'll teach them,' Roger said, taking the pumpkin off his head. 'Do you think we'll have any more tonight?'

'Yeah, perhaps one or two. Better get back in place.'

Halloween, greedy kids and disrespectful teenagers, what an annoying and pointless intrusion on everyone's lives. Begging for sweets, dressing up as ghouls, aliens and other unsightly monsters, why make something of an event that clearly does not teach children good moral standards? And what better way to confuse their tiny, underdeveloped minds than to spend all year saying, 'Don't eat that, it'll rot your teeth. You'll get fat,' and then every October allow them to gorge on as much junk food as they can possibly stomach. Where's the sense?

In years past we tried to ignore them, but they still came knocking, so we decided to put the fear of god into the little twerps so they would never come back. We may not be able to stop them from trespassing on our property, but we can build ourselves a reputation for a home not to be bothered with.

Then an egg smashed on the post by the steps, another splattered off the edging by the door. Wiping the egg from the side of my face, I yelled at the two teenaged cyclists at the end of our drive, 'We'll get you, you little bastards! Just you wait!'

Unfortunately, we still have to contend with the juvenile pranks of grown-ups. Halloween shouldn't be regarded as the eve before the feast of All Hallows or a festival for honouring the dead; it should be regarded as a day of amnesty for anarchy, chaos and everything associated with mayhem. I suppose it's revenge for having previously lost their wits when they were younger, but I can live with that so long as future generations are put off from calling at our door.

The neighbours don't like us much either. They blame us for the disappearance of that kid last year. Rumour has it that he went missing after running off scared from our home. They don't see it as their own fault. What kind of parent lets their child walk around in the middle of the night amongst disguised strangers? How can we be responsible for the actions of sick-minded individuals such as them? I suppose it will just have to happen again before they will come to realise the error of their ways.

I sat down with a cup of tea and switched on the box. To my disgust, I discovered that I was unable to escape Halloween, as the film of the same name was airing on channel four. I switched over to three and watched the news, listening to the depressing tales of despair that happened daily in the world outside my door. The familiar chime of a caller ringing the bell on my front porch soon disrupted my moment for solitude.

I opened the door and was greeted by a four-foot youth, covered by a white sheet. His unimaginative costume had but two eyeholes and hung above his knees. He appeared to be the shy type and waited for me to either give him some sweets or send him on his way.

'I think the line you need to recite is trick or treat.'

Suddenly, I felt rather cold. Roger was no longer on the porch. He hadn't come back in the house, so where could he be? The child was unmoving and silent.

'Look, kid, we don't do Halloween. Best try the Mason's next door. Did you hear me? We have no sweets. Go bother someone else.'

He remained steadfast and wordless. I leant down to his level and tried to look through his eyeholes. I could see nothing. Pissed off, I removed the sheet. I gasped in horror. There before me was a ghastly youth, pale and gaunt with blood running from his mouth. It was the missing boy from the year before and he wasn't wearing makeup.

Without warning, he hissed and presented me with a gaping smile to reveal a set of fangs and very sharp teeth. I toppled backwards into the hall, falling to the floor. I clambered upright and glanced back. To my surprise and relief, he was gone. I quickly shut the door and ran to the window. I looked about the garden and the drive. My appalling guest was nowhere to be seen. He had vanished.

Roger never returned and neither he nor the boy were ever found. To this day, I only leave the house during the day, and every year since, I always book a holiday abroad in October.

While We Were Out

'She's already eaten,' I said, 'but if she complains that she's hungry, she can have a snack before bed. Toast or cereal, but no chocolate. She can watch TV until eight o'clock, then get her to read you a story. She needs to be in bed by eight thirty at the latest. There's pop in the fridge and I've left a selection of crisps out for you on the counter. You have our number and if you have any problems, don't hesitate to call.'

'We'll be back before eleven,' my husband, Roger, added.

'Eight thirty to bed and no chocolate, got it,' Serafina said, as we put our coats on in the hallway.

'OK, I think we're ready. Ready?' Roger nodded. From the doorway I called out to our nine-year-old daughter, who was sitting in front of the TV.

'We're going now, Wendy. Be a good girl for Serafina.'

Wendy was too engrossed in her programme to reply.

'Everything will be fine, Mrs Redfern. Have a good night,' Serafina said as we stepped out of the door.

Nervously, I climbed into the passenger side of the car. I couldn't seem to get comfortable in my seat. Gazing into the wing mirror, I watched Serafina waving goodbye. As we pulled off the drive, she closed the door and I turned my attention to the way ahead.

'Do you think she'll be OK?'

'Yes,' Roger answered.

'How can you be so sure?'

'Look, just because it didn't work out with the last babysitter it doesn't mean that it won't with this one.'

I wasn't convinced, despite his reassuring glance. I felt anxious and my fretful manner continued even after we were seated at the restaurant.

'Will you please stop playing with your napkin?' Roger whispered. 'We're here to relax and enjoy ourselves, not to fret about our daughter and the babysitter. It's been three months since we last went out and you agreed to this, so will you at least pretend to be having a good time?'

I put the table napkin on my lap and picked up the menu. It was attractive and clearly labelled, but I couldn't focus on it. Unlike the napkin, I couldn't place my worries elsewhere. I needed reassurance.

'I need to call home,' I said laying the menu down. Roger watched me leave the table with a reluctant nod.

Standing in the entrance hall, I took my mobile phone out from my handbag and selected 'home' from the contacts list. I became more anxious with each ring, but my nervousness was swiftly eased once my call had been answered.

'Hello? Redfern residence, Serafina speaking.'

Breathing a sigh of relief, I replied, 'Hi, Serafina. I was just ringing to see if everything is alright.'

'Everything's fine, Mrs Redfern. I made Wendy some toast and now we're going to watch some TV together. Are you and Mr Redfern enjoying your night out?'

'Yes, great thanks. The restaurant's nice and we're just about to order. I'd better go. You and Wendy enjoy your show and I'll ring later. Thanks, Serafina.'

Back at our table, I found a waiter at Roger's side. Sitting down, I ordered and Roger watched me shuffle my chair closer to the table.

'And?' he asked taking a sip of water.

'Everything's fine. Wendy's watching TV and will be going to bed soon.'

'See? I told you it would be all right.'

'Yes, I can relax now, but I'll ring again before we leave.'

To my joy, I finally felt I could put my worries aside and embrace the peace and pleasurable surroundings. Roger and I were able to enjoy enticing food and stimulating conversation over the next two hours, which seemed to pass so freely. I felt contented, elated even, to the extent that I became flirtatious. It had been a wonderful night out and now I was eager to return home, but not for reasons of getting back to our daughter or for sleep.

Roger helped me with my coat as we prepared to leave. Taking my phone out from my handbag, I said, 'I'll just ring, Serafina to tell her that we're on our way.'

With my ear pressed to my mobile, I waited for her to answer my call. After seven rings the messaging service cut in and my stomach began to turn.

'She's not answering.'

'She's probably gone to the bathroom or she's in the kitchen making something to eat. Try again in the car.'

When Serafina didn't answer the phone on the journey home, the level of my heart rate rose and I had to hold onto the seat to stop myself shaking.

'Something's wrong,' I said. This time Roger didn't look so calm.

'I'm sure everything will be fine. Serafina will be sat on the sofa with her feet up, listening to her iPod. You know how young people are,' Roger said, concentrating on the road and trying to hide the waver in his voice.

We pulled into our drive. The lights were on, the curtains were drawn and the neighbourhood was peaceful, little preparation for what faced us inside.

I could hear the TV from the hallway, and the unmistakeable sound of the cartoon network.

Roger and I crept towards the living room. There was our daughter, sat in the middle of the room amongst a half dozen empty chocolate wrappers, with the babysitter lying next to her in a pool of blood.

'Oh my God!' I yelled, but in spite of my shriek, Wendy didn't turn around. Instead, she remained fixed on the TV and was as silent as the body beside her.

Roger went over to her and asked, 'Wendy, what happened?' She didn't answer.

At first I couldn't speak, but a few seconds later it all came out.

'Just look at the mess she's made. She's ruined the carpet. I'll never get any of this out. She's even got it on the sofa!'

'There's no need to worry about the sofa, it's leather, it will wipe clean. As for the carpet, well that's a write-off and we won't be able to claim this on the insurance. What concerns me is what I'm going to do with the body? I'm running out of garden space.'

'Why, Wendy, why?'

'I don't watch those kinds of programmes,' Wendy replied. 'I wanted to watch Super Snork, she wanted to watch West End Street. All that boring yakkity yak. She wouldn't change it back, so I went to the kitchen, got a knife and stabbed her. When she died, I figured that I was going to get into trouble anyway, so I ate the chocolate.'

'You got that right! You're grounded, you hear? Grounded!' I yelled. 'You can forget about seeing your friends or going to Cathy's birthday party next week and you won't be using the computer. All I asked was for you to be good for one night, one night, so that your dad and I could have an evening out. Go to your room. Mind the blood; I've got enough to clean as it is already. I've got to sit down.'

Six months later, the phone rang. Picking it up I said, 'Hello?'

'Yeah hi, my name is Bryga. I'm calling in response to the ad in the paper…'